# LITTLE BLUE MARBLE 2023

## WORLD ON FIRE

## EDITED BY KATRINA ARCHER

A Ganache Media Book

Vancouver

# LITTLE BLUE MARBLE
## 2023
### WORLD ON FIRE

*For Lahaina*

# CONTENTS

# INTRODUCTION

Welcome to the collected stories, essays, and poems of *Little Blue Marble* from 2023. All of these works are available for free online because *Little Blue Marble*'s mission is to educate and inspire, not to make a profit. We thank you, however, because your purchase of this anthology helps us bring the world more great stories about the climate crisis, and keeps our mission on track.

In 2023 it felt like the world, quite literally, started to burn. From the horrific fire that destroyed Lahaina and took far too many lives, to Europe where fires ripped through Italy, Spain, Portugal, and Greece, and my home country, Canada, where blazes in multiple provinces doubled the previous record of territory burned, it was hard to escape our new reality. Neither was Asia immune.

Billions of dollars of infrastructure lost. Countless lives taken and ruined. Wildlife and nature suffering at unprecedented scale.

And here we are, still subsidizing fossil fuel production on a global scale, with most governments likely nowhere close to hitting their carbon reduction commitments.

When smoke blanketed the east coast of North America, while I felt sorry for all the people living there, I have to admit a part of me thought "Finally." Finally, after a decade of living on the west coast and putting up with summers of smoke for weeks on end, finally, perhaps, the people in the country's power centres were getting a taste of what the rest of us now experience regularly. Finally, perhaps, they would get the message: this is what our lives will all be like unless you do something.

I somehow doubt it. But I can hope.

— *Katrina Archer, Publisher & Editor,* Little Blue Marble

# SNAIL TANK

## Monica Joyce Evans

THE restaurant was blue, like the whole place had been doused in artificial water, and Noma didn't like it. She clutched her purse as she followed the hostess, nodded to the staff as she passed. The CEO was in the back room surrounded by fish tanks: three giant panels that held back corals, eels, and other rarities. Somewhere in the biggest one a shark was turning. "They're not for eating," he said as she approached. "I don't eat anywhere that serves meat."

Noma sat in the chair that had been pulled out for her. "I appreciate your time." She kept her gloves on, and her purse.

"I'm interested in solutions." The CEO's smile was warm and charming, practiced. Four other people at the table gathered up materials, slid out in silence. "All solutions. Unorthodox is my orthodoxy."

"You've done so much good already," Noma said. Flattery was always a good opener.

The CEO leaned back in his chair. "So, what's your plan

to save the world?"

Noma took a breath, listened to the reassuring hum of the systems around her, protecting those little pockets of plasticless ocean. "I don't have one. But I can save Waikiki Beach."

He waited. Those sands were underwater, of course, right up to the doorframes of those expensive old hotels. "It starts with corals," Noma went on. "Reefs, shorelines, tide pools. We work with shallow ecosystems."

"I'm familiar," the CEO said. People appeared and patterned the table with small plates of food, vegan and inscrutable, smelling like sea foam.

"My apologies." Noma opened her purse. Carefully, she pulled out a small, plexiglass container which held a single shell: glossy, tapered, and whorled with intricate patterns as if it had been tattooed. In the restaurant's lighting, it looked brown. "This is *conus lecanoscopus*." Noma opened the lid. "A cone snail. And it's going to save the ocean."

"Explain."

She swallowed. "Cone snails are weird. They're predators, they eat fish, but of course they can't swim after them. They use venom instead." He was staring at the blue expanse over her shoulder, fingers tapping. "But cone snails move fast, evolutionarily speaking. They adapt specific venoms to specific prey animals almost on the fly, because processes in their DNA let them adapt instantaneously to new environments. My company knows how they do it. And we can use that knowledge to save whole ecosystems."

She had his attention again. "You're going to teach ecosystems to evolve faster?"

"On a planetary scale, it's already happening." Noma put one gloved finger on the back of the beautiful shell. "With cone snail DNA, we can keep up with it."

The CEO reached out as if to touch the shell also, thought better of it. "Congratulations. Of all the pitches I've heard today, yours is the most mad scientist."

She would not say the word unorthodox. "You should meet the Antarctic shelf guys," she said instead. "I think they're working on a freeze ray."

The CEO picked up something lichenous from his plate with a pair of chopsticks, dipped it in pale foam. Noma hadn't been brought a plate, she realized. "So cone snail DNA is going to save the world," the CEO said. "What do you need?"

"Testing," Noma said. "It's a question of activating a particular set of gene sequences. We know where it is in cone snails, and where to find it in fifteen other species, mostly crustaceans, some fish. I need a piece of ocean for large-scale testing of our more viable subjects."

"You want to release mutating fish into the ocean?"

She looked down, willing him to see how stupid the idea was. "So they can survive the next fifty years, yes. Because of this little guy." She picked up the snail, held it out so he could see the mottled pattern, like an enigma. "See?"

He took it. "Well, it's a bold proposal." He turned the shell over. Sucked in his breath.

"It's just the shell," Noma lied. The CEO put it down, prodded the small red mark at the base of his palm. "The inner edge is serrated. No snail in there."

"Fascinating." The CEO rubbed his palm. "Really interesting proposal." He stood up, but didn't extend his hand.

"Thank you so much," Noma rose also. "For hearing me out." She slid the snail back into its container and smiled her way outside.

On her way out, she passed a pair of nervous young men in expensive suits, chattering about mycelium. Whatever they were asking for, they'd get it, as the CEO became increasingly warm, comfortably emotional. *Conus lecanoscopus* was one of Noma's favourites. Venomous, yes, but it made its prey happy, complacent, and perfectly content to loll around in front of the beautiful thing that might eat it one day.

As soon as the restaurant was out of sight, she made the call. "One group in front of you," she said. "Make sure you're with him in twenty minutes, make your ask in twenty-five. Get it in writing. Show him the plastic collection drones, he'll think they're adorable. And don't forget the antivenin, or he'll say yes to everyone after you too." She hung up.

Save the world, indeed. Lots of people had crazy ideas, but Noma would make sure the CEO's billions went to the right one. Not freeze rays or magic cone snail DNA, but ideas that actually had a chance in hell of working. Anything else was just too risky. "Well done, sleepyhead," she said to the snail. "Looks like you're going to save the world after all."

# ABOUT THE AUTHOR

Monica Joyce Evans is a digital game designer and researcher who also writes speculative fiction. Her short fiction has appeared in multiple publications including *Analog*, *Nature: Futures*, and *DreamForge*. She lives in North Texas with her husband, two daughters, and approximately ten million books. You can reach her at monicajoyceevans@gmail.com.

# MICROCLIMATES OF THE RICH AND FAMOUS

## R. K. Duncan

ON *today's episode, the breathtaking Salish-Pacifica estate of Darien Walton-Musk, biogeneering pioneer and microretail magnate. We'll speak with Walton-Musk and his architect/companion AI, Pacifica, later in the program, but first enjoy the beautiful landscape of the grounds.*

*The border of Salish-Pacifica is understated, beginning with the five kilometre mist belt, where vapour sprinklers seed the air and soil with desalinated reclaimed water to reduce fire risk and maintain the estate at historical mid-twentieth-century humidity. Beyond the mist, the world's largest remaining contiguous redwood forest rises a hundred metres into the always blue and partly cloudy sky. Walton-Musk has remained coy about the proportion of biogeneered FastRed™ trees among the transplanted old-growth specimens, and our horticultural consultants assure us they can't tell the difference.*

*We'll pass over the sprawling 114-room mansion of local redwood and Italian marble for now to look at this astonishing expanse of beach and blue lagoon. The white sand is imported from Grand Cayman, because the reef of proprietary nanocoral that keeps the water calm and Caribbean blue doesn't produce any waste except the desalinated water fueling those misters farther inland. Salish-Pacifica is one of only three estates with a Walton-Musk proprietary reef, and he's keeping this treasure close to the chest, so much so that we won't be able to bring you any dive-cam footage today.*

• • •

There is a special peacefulness to sailing, to moving on the water under no power but the wind. It's like what I imagine weightlessness to be. I first experienced it as a child, a long time ago, when summer vacations and the middle class and the coast of Maine were still undebatable things, and the feeling of wonder that found me on a friend of a friend's boat then has never fully left. There is a magic in the windblown quiet of a sailboat that removes me from the chaos of the sinking world, especially on a day like today, when the brilliant sun shines like silver and glass on the wave tips and the steady wind keeps the air swept clean.

I hated to ruin the feeling with that bootlicking vidcast, but I had been hoping for an uncensored shot of the reef and the defenses on Salish-Pacifica's sea approach. As much as I love it, I'm not a stunt sailor, and any intel on getting past the layers of surveillance and defense between me and that beach would help. I'll have to trust the wind Walton-Musk's atmospheric fuckery maintains to suck me in and keep

*Heartstopper* on course, and on the adversarial pixel-patterns on the sail to crash the surveillance AI once I come into camera range.

Apart from that little interlude with the propaganda stream, these last weeks working *Heartstopper* slowly up the coast, laying up on rarely surveilled beaches, taking wide swings around commercial ports and standard flight paths to try and keep off camera as much as possible, had been the most peaceful of my life. And it felt good to know I was doing something.

The quiet and the brightness and the steady wind off the deep ocean turn from idyllic to *Silent Spring* as I come closer to Salish-Pacifica's lagoon. All the salt, oil, heavy metals, microplastics—everything that nanocoral filters out—are discharged on the ocean side, building up faster than the current can clear away. The dead zone's about three kilometres out from the reef now, seven years after construction, and it's growing all the time. You could believe he didn't know about it, if you didn't know the lagoon is just the right size for the dead zone to be over the horizon from Walton-Musk's favourite lounge spot on the beach. As it is, he's already poisoned ten times the lagoon's area into somewhere even a red tide can't live, and it's only going to keep spreading as long as his reef's there.

The swell over the smart-reef is barely visible but the stark change in the water colour to shocking Caribbean blue makes it obvious. The white-sand beach and the craggy hill behind it rise to display that absurd Fabergé egg of a mansion like a postcard from a better world. Even before I sighted the highest turret, cameras were tracking *Heartstopper*, calculating heading and assessing threat.

Even knowing how to look, I can barely make out the camouflaged drones taking off as I slide through one of the channels in the reef, or feel the net of nanosensors when it tastes my skin. That's what it takes to keep paradise private these days, while the West burns and the delta drowns and winter retreats for good under the midnight sun. You could never bring a weapon to this poison paradise. Unless of course the defenses could deliver it for you.

I only get past the reef because the sail worked well enough that a kill order's waiting on the individual drones scanning *Heartstopper*. I expect a dozen different warning systems are blaring alarm somewhere inside, and live security will be scrambling, but command and control's still rebooting. That means the nanonet can't talk to the drones, so they need to triple check there aren't any volatiles, secret explosives, or spring-loaded herbicides sent by a jealous rival, waiting to be aerosolized when they burn *Heartstopper* to the waterline and sink her body for the reef to eat. That gives me time to bring her where she needs to be and jump.

I hit the water, and it's perfect swimming temperature, just a little cold, but not so much I couldn't spend hours floating. It feels clean on my skin, cleaner than anything natural I've touched for years. Shows what nanotech can do, I guess.

I'm only a few strokes from *Heartstopper* when the drones

start blasting, close enough my brain would pulp from the concussion if they hit below the water line, but thankfully Walton-Musk's security is all airborne, so they dismantle *Heartstopper* from above and give me time to swim clear. His security will probably pick me up when I get to shore, but I've already done the job.

We killed most of the real coral reefs without trying, just one more casualty of cascading collapse and warming water, but destroying Walton-Musk's monstrosity took work. Dozens of biologists and gene-pirates spent two years in the lab to build a deadly Trojan horse into the trees' DNA and three more in the nursery bootlegging Walton-Musk's own tech to speed-grow them tall enough for timber. Add to that least thirty shipbuilders, professional hobbyists who could put our three ships together outside a corporate shipyard, and three sailing bums, willing to spend the weeks at sea and bring the payloads in all at the same time to choke the poison coral and return the coast to nature.

The reef will die beyond replacement as it digests *Heartstopper*, and spread a self-destructing virus to anything that touches it. I'll probably be shot and dumped if Walton-Musk or his goons realize what's happening while they still have me, but there's a chance they'll just hand me to local law enforcement for a beating and hotbox cell, or set me walking barefoot out into the badlands. I've got exfil plans if I can get that far, but it doesn't matter. The damage is done. No more dead zone. No more blue lagoon. No more water for those misters that let him pretend the world isn't burning down around him. Pity about the redwoods, but they might still survive when the next wildfire crosses the dried-out mist belt. Maybe I'll still be around to see that.

# ABOUT THE AUTHOR

R. K. Duncan is a fat queer polyamorous wizard and author of fantasy, horror, and occasional sci-fi. He writes from a few rooms of a venerable West Philadelphia row home, where he dreams of travel and the demise of capitalism. His other full-time job is keeping house for himself and his live-in partner. Before settling on writing, he studied linguistics and philosophy at Haverford college. He attended Viable Paradise 23 in 2019. His occasional musings and links to other work can be found at rkduncan-author.com.

# THE SMILING VIROLOGIST

## Dan Peacock

Dan Peacock

*SAMUEL BURNS is a tall, thin man who seems nervous in front of the cameras. He fiddles with the wire linking the mic that is clipped onto his shirt, and one foot taps quietly but frantically on the floor as he talks.*

SAMUEL: I suppose you want to talk about what happened to Adam Lewinsky, how he became the Smiling Virologist. I just want to say, though, for the record, I don't like that moniker. It makes him sound like the Joker, or something. To me, he's just Adam. And besides, history might be kind to him. Maybe it'll turn out that he was right. Maybe ACID will turn out to be the pandemic that saved us.

I met him in the late thirties, *my* late thirties, in fact, when I started a new job at his lab. After COVID there was a lot of new funding for virology and vaccinology, a lot of positions, but a lot of competition, too. There was a real sense of guardianship in working on preventing the next pandemic.

Adam had done his doctorate on animals that provoked unusual nervous responses in humans. *Carukia barnesi* was one of his favourites. It was a jellyfish whose sting could bring on a sense of impending doom, and cause the victim to feel certain that they were going to die. He'd been stung while handling one, once, and his eyes had glazed over while he tried and failed to describe the sense of overwhelming existential dread. Far more excruciating than the actual pain.

*Samuel shudders and crosses his arms.*

He talked about bufo toads, too, that caused hallucinogenic reactions if eaten or licked. A caterpillar whose toxins caused brain haemorrhages. A subspecies of wandering spider whose venom made you permanently impotent, if you didn't die of asphyxiation in the hours following the bite.

I'm probably building a picture of some wispy-haired mad scientist. That's not right—kooky is probably the word. Besides, he was bald. Adam was a great guy. As much as he loved to wax on about his own research and projects, about the potential uses of animal by-products in making the next vaccines, he'd always find time to help me, and always volunteered as a sounding board to bounce ideas off of. Adam was happy, and dedicated to his work. The Green Death changed that.

•  •  •

*In archive footage, ADAM LEWINSKY is somber, pale, and looks like he hasn't slept properly in years. The buttons on his shirt are misaligned; one buttonhole missed on the left side, the spare fabric buckling out on the right. His fingernails are chewed and ragged.*

ADAM: It was our worst nightmare. Something with the R rate of measles, multiple transmission methods, and the mortality rate of Ebola. Our most conservative models, even with the entire world put back on lockdown, put the potential deaths at over a billion within two years. It would have made COVID look like a Sunday drive. But we were lucky, or blessed, or something else. Just like what happened with Omicron, it mutated into a far less lethal but much more transmissible form, and burned itself out in a year. Half the world was infected and only a hundred million died. God. Only.

*Lewinsky shakes his head.*

I didn't believe it when I heard it, either, that it had been engineered. That someone had made it on purpose. They never caught the guy, but his manifesto said that he was trying to cull the global population. "For environmental reasons." God. *[Expletive]* maniac. We're handling the climate crisis about as well as a planet full of self-serving primates can do, which is to say, not at all, but there had to be a better way than that. There had to be.

• • •

*Someone has brought SAMUEL BURNS a cup of coffee and he sits back, taking a sip. The mug scrapes against the mic pinned to his shirt and he winces at the sound, putting the mug down on a little table next to his chair.*

Sorry. As I was saying, the Green Death changed him.

Virologists had had our moment in the spotlight, dealing with COVID and the minor pandemics that came after it. And although we fixed the Green Death, too, it was one of *us* that started it in the first place. Whoever it was. We were under a lot more scrutiny after that, and a lot more pressure.

Adam retreated into his work, but he still found time to talk to me. He was growing increasingly *[expletive]* about the climate crisis, what with the wildfires in northern Europe and Canada, and what happened with the Netherlands and the Union of Pacific Nations. He came close to saying the guy who'd come up with the Green Death had a point, but I knew that's not what he meant. He just wanted to find a vaccine for the planet, the same way we did for all the newest diseases.

I suppose you know where this is going.

• • •

*ELLEN KENNEDY's suit is almost as formal as her hair is informal, a shock of bright dyed blue that matches her tie and earrings. She holds herself in a way that only professional newsreaders and broadcasters can.*

ELLEN: As the first reports came in, I was scared, reading them out on the air. It seemed so familiar, and so soon after the Green Death. Every time there was a new case of a mystery illness, you had to ask yourself if this was the big one. This time, a whole city was infected with some new unidentified disease, and thousands upon thousands of people were hospitalized. Debilitating nausea, rabid discomfort, painful rashes, lucid delusions of impending doom. Nurses on duty were saying they'd not seen suffering like it outside of the cancer wards. It started popping up all across the globe, despite the strictest quarantines in recorded history, and I was terrified.

But after a few days of misery the symptoms seemed to clear, and there were virtually no deaths. And it got stranger. People started putting two and two together. Vegetarians and vegans weren't affected. Nor pescatarians. Neither were people who just ate poultry as their main source of meat. It was beef and pork. People were becoming violently, excruciatingly intolerant to certain meats. We were scrambling for answers, and then Adam Lewinsky made his broadcast.

*KENNEDY grimace-smiles.*

It turned out, funnily enough, it had already been up on YouTube for weeks. It's just that Adam only had six followers, to start with, and none of them noticed straightaway. The algorithm hadn't pushed it to the front.

*Cut to footage from partway through LEWINSKY's video.*

ADAM: But of course, it's unavoidable. Methane from livestock is the number one accelerant of climate change, especially now that the use of fossil fuels and petrol cars have been scaled back. We could slow the runaway effect, maybe to a crawl, if we went fully plant-based. Give a few more generations a chance on this planet. But people just aren't ready to give up meat, and particularly beef. Livestock takes up nearly 90% of viable agricultural land, and the vast majority of that is for bovine herds. That land could feed ten times the amount of people if used more efficiently, too. Or just given back to nature. Think of the forests that could grow, all the carbon that could be soaked up!

*Cut back to ELLEN KENNEDY.*

ELLEN: Look how giddy he is while he's explaining. I hate the stupid boogeyman name, but you can see where the media got the idea for it. The Smiling Virologist. Every parent, I think, will recognise that look. He's a child proudly showing you something he's made.

ADAM: I'd worked with *Amblyomma americanum*, the lone star tick, in the past. The really interesting thing about *americanum* is that its bite often triggers a permanent allergy to a certain sugar molecule, alpha-gal. This molecule is present in both the saliva of the tick itself, and also certain meats.

ELLEN: He does look somewhat like a mad scientist here, I will concede.

ADAM: The virus I created had an impossibly high transmission rate, but no symptoms or side effects. In truth, you would never even know you had it … until you ate meat. At that point, you'd suffer a few unpleasant side effects for a few days. Nothing fatal. Just unpleasant.

ELLEN: "A few unpleasant side effects." Jesus. I'm a flexitarian, so I was lucky enough to avoid ACID's effects until they figured out what was triggering them, but my partner had it. He said he wanted to die from the nausea, and there was something in his head telling him the world was going to end. And Lewinsky says there was nothing fatal about ACID? A lot of coroners disagree.

*The camera zooms in slightly as ELLEN pauses to gather her thoughts.*

And yet, just like that, almost overnight, the entire world was either aggressively allergic to meat, or so scared of the side effects that they didn't bother with it any more anyway. He's got a lot of fanboys, don't get me wrong. But there's also a lot of very angry people out there who want to speak to him.

*ELLEN hesitates, listening to a question off-camera.*

Am I? I don't know. I think it's too early to say what he's done. A lot of people have gone through a lot because of what he did. My husband isn't the same. I'm not sure I am, either.

*ELLEN exhales deeply.*

And I'd kill for a proper burger.

• • •

*SAMUEL BURNS is shifting in his seat, uncomfortable.*

Look, I don't know. People have largely moved to poultry since the outbreak of ACID, and lab-grown meat that doesn't contain alpha-gal has boomed in popularity. Some people are starting to say that McDonalds tastes like it used to again. We've not really seen a rise in vegetarianism or veganism, though. Despite that, even on its own the switch to poultry is a net benefit. I know cows were supposed to be the pollutingest thing left on the planet.

And obviously they aren't breeding them any more, but what will happen to the last generation, the cows and pigs that are alive now? They'll probably get ground down into feed for the other animals we can still eat. And what about the farmers?

I'm not an atmospheric scientist. I think it's too early to see how far methane levels will really drop, though. We won't know what Adam has done for a good few years. I just wonder if he's out there somewhere, waiting to see for himself.

*SAMUEL strains to hear a question from off-camera.*

No, we're not working on a cure for ACID. And that's not a moral or environmental decision. It's not really killing people, and there are plenty of things that are. We have bigger fish that need frying.

*SAMUEL smiles.*

And certainly not beef.

• • •

*At the time of broadcast, Adam Lewinsky is still unaccounted for.*

*Two thousand deaths have been attributed to Alpha-gal Complex Immune Disease (ACID), but these figures are contested by the World Health Organisation.*

*Since the outbreak, global beef consumption has dropped by 96%. Pork consumption has dropped by 94%.*

*Relative to pre-ACID levels, annual methane emissions have decreased by 30% and are still falling.*

# ABOUT THE AUTHOR

Dan Peacock is a sci-fi and fantasy writer from the UK. His short stories have been published or are forthcoming in *F&SF*, *Kaleidotrope*, and *Etherea*, and he is also a first reader for *Orion's Belt*. You can find links to all his published stories at danpeacockwriter.com, and he tweets at @DanPeacock92.

# RISING DEATH

## C. J. Carter-Stephenson

THE killer to be,
Her infinitely varied blues
Muted to black
By the midnight sky,
Dances slowly, rhythmically
Along the shoreline,
Singing a gentle lullaby
To the deserted dunes.
Beautiful, hypnotic display
Hard to reconcile
With her tempest temper,
When welcoming arms
Become hammers of destruction,
Sending swimmers and fishermen
Scurrying for cover.
She is the ocean,
Symbol of the cycles

Of the natural world.
Seemingly constant,
Yet subtly changing,
Left unchecked,
She could swallow the world.

The politician,
Cadaver-thin vulture
With talon fingers,
Paces his study in City Hall,
Bulbous eyes glued
To a flickering TV,
Listening with disdain
As scientists rant—
Criticize, spread their lies—
Sanctimonious drivel
For impressionable fools.
Enemies should be known,
But he's heard enough,
Stabs at his remote
To cut them off.
He closes the curtains
On a record snowfall
That has turned
The city glistening white,
Flops into an armchair
With a glass of port.
Climate change does not exist!

Who would win in a wrestling match—
Man or water?

# ABOUT THE AUTHOR

C. J. Carter-Stephenson is a UK writer, who was born in the county of Essex and currently lives on the Isle of Wight. He holds an MA in Creative Writing from the University of Southampton, has been a Writers of the Future finalist, and has had three books published. Other publication credits include stories and/or poems in *Aesthetica, Möbius, Writers Muse, AE: The Canadian Science Fiction Review, Speculative North, Youth Imagination, Dark Horizons, The Fifth Di...* And *Illumen*. He is also the narrator of Back of the Bookshelf, a monthly podcast of classic genre fiction.

# I THINK THAT I SHALL NEVER SEE

## Stephen Kotowych

GOOD afternoon, fellow tree lovers, and welcome to the North American Biosphere Tree Museum. My name is Aliah —I'll be your guide today.

Step through the airlock and we'll begin the tour. Please feel free to ask questions at any time.

Our museum houses the most extensive collection of preproprietary tree species in the world. We are affiliated with several sister biospheres around the globe, but we are the only one designated a UNESCO World Heritage Site.

Most trees in our collection are extinct in the wild as nonmodified organisms. They've been outcompeted by their designer-engineered cousins or by entirely novel transgenic species.

While the observation decks are sealed off from the forest

galleries, the decontamination showers you took and the jumpsuits you're wearing are just some of the ways we try to ensure no genetically modified pollen, seeds, or organisms enter the museum and pollute our collection.

The biocontainment procedures we use are similar to those in Level 4 microbiology labs, where the world's deadliest diseases are studied.

You'll have noticed the rush of wind when entering the museum. All airlocks maintain positive pressure, ensuring no foreign organisms enter. Outside air drawn for ventilation, and all air within the facility cycles through a series of HEPA and electrostatic filters to scrub the air of pollen or spores before being sterilized with UV-C light.

If you follow me, we'll head up to the observation deck.

Looking into the enclosure, you'll see over 200 species of trees growing in sealed galleries of varying climates. All our trees are native to North America, and all are in their natural, unmodified states.

Our arbourists—you can see some there, working under that American chestnut—tend the trees full-time. No, it's OK, kiddo, you can wave to them!

Our team deals with any ailment befalling our trees, from fungal infections to root rot. You can imagine how catastrophic an infestation of longhorn beetles would be. Or an outbreak of leaf blight.

Yes—a question? No, ma'am, I'm afraid the tour doesn't include an excursion into any of the enclosures. Physical access to the trees is tightly controlled. Our arbourists sign on for three- to six-month tours of duty working with the collection. To avoid contamination, they undergo a rigorous (and rather unpleasant) decon procedure to flush their bodies—inside and out—of foreign and GM organisms before being sealed inside the enclosure.

Down this corridor is our central laboratory. Through these windows, you can see our tree biologists hard at work saving North America's native trees.

In the racks under those purple lights, trees grow from seeds and cuttings. Some will eventually find a home in our museum forest. Others are destined for use in reclamation projects across the continent.

One of our most urgent projects is the common sugar maple. The modified version—which makes three times the sap of a natural maple—is so prevalent in the wild that we're having a hard time locating unmodified specimens for our collection.

The GM maple tends to explode during winter cold snaps when its sap freezes and expands—meaning soon the entire maple sugar industry could become extinct, along with the tree.

In our historical exhibits, you can learn the progression of genetic modification in trees.

Most of the early changes produced taller trees or faster-growing ones, primarily for logging. Some trees were modified to grow straighter, or with fewer branches, or to have increased density, again primarily for industrial harvesting.

Later, the inclusion of entirely novel genes became commonplace for consumer GM trees—the kind of thing found today at your local garden centre. Perhaps you have a Topiary Tree™ in your front yard or a Bonsai Tree™ on your desk.

The best-known consumer tree is, of course, the Christmas Tree™. Jellyfish genes impart the mature needles with bioluminescence, making the tree self-lighting.

But the most famous—or should I say *infamous*—achievement in GM trees is the gTree™. It's had a devastating impact on the natural habitat of the trees preserved in our collection.

The culmination of the agrifood giant Santamondo Inc.'s genetically modified tree project, the gTree™ is basically a Japanese Black Pine with genes from several African tree species, like the Miombo and the African Brown Olive tree, which give it fire- and drought-resistance, and the ability to propagate quickly, even in bare and rocky ground.

At first, the gTree™ was used in carbon-capture projects around the world. But gTree™ seeds quickly spread into the wild thanks to wind and wildlife. And once they did, well ...

gTrees™ grew faster and in more places than other tree species, choking out native vegetation in dozens of countries.

In California, annual wildfires let the gTree™ spread unchecked once other vegetation had burned away. If you go to the San Bernadino Mountains these days, all you'll see are the characteristic tufts of gTree™ foliage.

Santamondo Inc. was upset about their proprietary

organisms getting loose. But thanks to a series of favourable court decisions, Santamondo's solution—charging a technology licensing fee to anyone found with a wild gTree™ on their property—was upheld.

Under this precedent, Santamondo later charged the owners of *any* plants found to have patented gTree™ genes inherited through cross-pollination.

You'll recall that these fees assessed on Central Park eventually bankrupted New York City.

Part of our conservation efforts include lobbying world governments to change laws and hold agricultural biotech corporations responsible for environmental damage caused by products like the gTree™. But international laws on trade, technology, and liability aren't on our side.

As you can imagine, this is a very lengthy, very costly process, and we can't do it without the help and financial assistance of concerned citizens like you. Our museum is a registered charity, and donations are always welcome.

Another way you can help is by purchasing some of the lovely items we have for sale in our boutique, and so if you'll follow me, the final stop of our tour will be the gift shop ...

# ABOUT THE AUTHOR

Stephen Kotowych is a winner of the Writers of the Future Grand Prize, Spain's Ictineu Award, and is a two-time finalist for Canada's Aurora Award. His stories have appeared in *Interzone*, *IGMS*, numerous anthologies, and been translated into a dozen languages. His collection of short stories, *Seven Against Tomorrow*, is available now. He hosts a podcast about the life and times of Nikola Tesla, and enjoys guitar, tropical fish, and writing about himself in the third person. Visit his website at www.kotowych.com.

# THE CHRYSALIS

## Don Redwood

"You don't actually believe all that do you?"

"You're such a baby!"

"Caterpillars don't become butterflies."

"The adults just switch them when you're not looking, you idiot."

"Magic's for babies."

"Leave her alone! You'll ruin it for her."

"Maybe you'll turn into a big smelly cockroach!"

Loz tried to look away, but her cousins were circled round her. She bit her lip and frowned, trying to shelter her excitement from their taunts and laughter.

She thought about the caterpillar she'd been given at school that day. It was so tiny she'd been too scared to touch it. It hadn't eaten the big leaf in its jar, so she'd gone exploring in the greenhouse and come back with some elderflowers. She knew they would be tasty, but the caterpillar didn't touch them either. It just wriggled along its twig doing

"

silly dances. None of the other children's caterpillars were eating either. Miss Carruthers said not to worry—caterpillars don't like being watched—they would eat everything up once the children were back down in their bunks.

Miss Carruthers wouldn't lie to her. Would she?

"Aww don't cry!"

"I was joking! You won't really turn into a cockroach."

• • •

The leaf and flowers were all gone the next day. So was the caterpillar. In place of the squirming noodle of yellow and green stripes, Loz found a shiny blob, hanging from the twig like a little leaf bud. It felt crispy when she stroked it, but Miss Carruthers said not to touch them too much because they were so delicate.

It was a chrysalis, she learned. The middle stage between caterpillar and butterfly.

It was pretty, but it didn't do very much. The class spent their excitement making butterfly stencils and decorating some of the dingy corridors beneath their classroom with colourful butterfly prints.

Loz joined in, but she couldn't stop thinking about what her cousins had said. The way the caterpillar had changed suddenly overnight did seem suspicious. She was afraid to ask Miss Carruthers about it, in case she got in trouble, so she came up with another plan.

Insects turning into other insects was the most magical thing they had learned at school so far, but it wasn't the only magical thing. There was also magnets—magic metals that pushed and pulled each other without touching. They had even made their own hands magnetic one day by dipping them in tubs of magnetic paint.

While the other kids painted even more butterfly stencils, Loz snuck into the class store cupboard. She stole a splodge of magnetic paint—just enough to cover her chrysalis, which was the same colour anyway. When her butterfly hatched, she would test it with a magnet. If it didn't stick, her cousins were right—the adults were just pretending.

• • •

Loz's butterfly was the most beautiful thing she had ever seen. It was mostly purple, but there were other colours scattered around like bits of broken glass. Probably every colour from the rainbow was there. And it was perfectly symmetrical.

They were supposed to name them. Loz had come up with the name "Hope," but she would only use it if her experiment worked out.

It was standing on the twig, flapping its wings, but not fast enough to actually fly. Loz took her magnet from her school bag and opened the jar. Her heart was going so fast it felt like it might fly instead of the butterfly.

She touched the magnet against its wings. They snapped shut, flattened against the invisible pull of the magnet. Loz shouted "Yes!" so loud she was worried all the other children would look round, but they were too distracted by their own butterflies.

Then Loz noticed Hope was making a strange buzzing

noise, like the lights in her and her cousins' bunkroom. Loz pulled Hope free from the magnet in case it was hurting her, taking care not to damage her delicate wings, and did a big sigh of relief when the noise stopped. But something was wrong. Hope wasn't moving. Loz watched, her mouth open in disbelief, praying for Hope to flap her wings, unsure whether two or two million seconds had passed before she started crying.

When the children took their jars to the greenhouse to let their butterflies loose, Loz was still standing there. Miss Carruthers came over and Loz told her everything that had happened.

"Don't worry, Loz. Your cousins were right—we do swap the insects between classes. The only reason the magnet worked was because your butterfly is actually made of metal. You haven't killed anything! Your magnet must have broken its electrics."

Loz stared at Miss Carruthers as she processed this information. First she felt relieved, but then, really angry. How could her teacher of all people just lie to her like that? Then she felt worried—maybe Miss Carruthers was only lying now to make her feel better, and she had killed her butterfly after all.

"You shouldn't learn this for a few years, so don't tell your classmates, but butterflies went extinct along with all the bigger animals. We have some frozen eggs, but we won't activate them until the earth has healed. In the meantime, we need these robotic ones to pollinate our plants. We pretend to children they are alive because although losing this belief one day will be painful, it's an important kind of pain. It stops the Big Extinction from becoming some meaningless story. So we can learn from it, and when we finally get back out there, we will have evolved as a species."

Loz cried all the way to the greenhouse room. She was proud to know the truth, but she also wished she was as happy and carefree as the other children. Still, she smiled to see the greenhouse alive with dozens of electric butterflies. In their colourful, fluttery dance, she could almost imagine Hope was there.

# ABOUT THE AUTHOR

Don Redwood lives in Glasgow, Scotland. He likes cycling, wildlife gardening, juggling, and imagining future and alternate worlds. He has just finished writing his first novel about mental health and the climate crisis, stretching from the present day into a supposedly utopian near future. His short stories have previously appeared in *Daily Science Fiction* and *Mycelia*. He is a member of the friendly but ruthless Glasgow Science Fiction Writer's Circle. Find out more at donredwood.com.

# FLAVOURS OF A MEMORY

## Catherine Weaver

MISTS *lie over the craggy rocks just off the shore. Sea gulls cry, sea lions bark, kelp crunches underfoot.*

*Cypress and sage bend in the breeze coming off the ocean.*

*Purple wildflowers peek out from dry brown grass. A bent oak shelters crows.*

*A peek into the secluded life of a tidepool: sea anemones, sea weed, tiny crabs, and mussels all live within.*

*A jogger and her dog run by, frisbee thrown ahead and brought back eagerly, to be thrown again.*

Carli sighs and stops the digital recording of her grandmother's walk on the beach. She shouldn't use precious generated electricity to run it, but it's her lifeline to what was.

Her grandmother promised her that what once was could be again, and she has to believe it. She holds on to that promise to get her through the day.

She carefully puts the equipment away, and unseals the dome door to check on the tidal generators at her beach, many yards inland of her grandmother's once-pristine Monterey Bay.

She slides her ancient brown boat from the cracked brown shore into the tepid brown waves, and rows out to pull garbage flotsam from the generators.

There are no bird cries, only the desultory slosh of soapy waves under a tan sky.

After rowing her haul back to the shore, carting it to the disposal ditch, and tossing it into the abyss, she checks the desalinization and filter mechanisms, holding her breath against the stench.

That smell won't last forever. What once was will be again. Her grandmother promised. There are better days ahead.

Once she's washed the filth from her hands, she unseals the large vegetable dome and takes a deep breath of rich, moist air. The dome's filled with life: butterflies, bees, earthworms, and all the vegetables her grandmother grew from her hoarded heritage seeds.

When plant disease ripped across the world, her grandmother's seeds became the only food for miles. The disease destroyed all the single-species wheat, corn, potatoes, tomatoes, safflower, rice, oats, and alfalfa in the world in one year—the same year that the Northern Hemisphere's major water reservoirs dried up.

Her grandmother didn't talk much about those days, and Carli never asked. Somehow she and Grandpa and a few other families built, maintained, and grew the farms, and turned hell into paradise.

Carli moves into that paradise now, feeling the reverence and joy she always does in the vegetable dome.

Today it's time to train the new peas. Kneeling in the soil, she wraps a vine carefully around its trellis, hooking its fingers tenderly around diamond-shaped supports. It's the child she never had, the future of her race, the hope of continuing life.

The door unseals with a puff of air, and Ty enters, the floppy felt hat she made for him last Christmas covering his curly brown hair. "Someone came back from New Mexico, and you'll never guess what they brought in exchange for the sweet potato starts we sent them."

Carli's heart beats faster. She wants to run screaming with glee out to the gate, but she carefully stands and walks, with the respect for all living things in the dome that her grandmother taught her.

When she gets to the wagon behind the solar jeepney that made the thousand-mile trek, her breath catches.

*Maize!*

Piles and piles of rainbow-coloured dried ears of maize fill the wagon. Enough to cultivate half a farming dome. She's never seen maize in real life—only pictures—and here it is, enough for everyone in the Monterey farm and all their descendants to eat maize every day, after the first planting season.

"Thank you," she says to the New Mexican. "You're welcome to our home for as long as you'd like to stay. Florie in Dome Three over there will help you get settled."

When the man is a little way away she turns to her husband. "Ty! Let's do something wicked! Let's waste a little of this gift!"

Ty raises his eyebrows, but then narrows his eyes and grins. "What do you have in mind, my love?"

She grabs three ears off the top of the wagon and runs toward home. "Come on and you'll see!"

When they're inside their dome, she plonks a lidded pan on the table. "Rub all the kernels off the maize and put them in this pan."

She holds an ear and demonstrates for him, and they cover the pan bottom with a rainbow of maize beads. Then she turns on the griddle.

"I know it's a sin to waste seeds and power like this, but I've been wanting to do this since I was three, when Grandma showed me a recording of it."

"I don't know what you're doing, Carli, but you deserve to waste a little. I don't remember the last time I've seen you so excited."

She covers the pan and sets it on the griddle. The first *pop* pushes her heart up into her throat. But she recognizes her cue and shakes the pan as hard and fast as she can. More shots ring out within the pan, until there's a whole fusillade going on in there.

And then it slows.

She turns off the power and removes the pan to a trivet on the table.

"Behold!" She whips the lid off and a rich, full aroma hits their nostrils. *"Popcorn!"*

Ty gazes at the pile of pastel blooms. "What do we do with it?"

"This!" She grabs a handful and shoves it into her mouth.

Flavours of memories she never knew envelop her. Each satisfying crunch releases a new aroma into the back of her throat, filling her head with warmth and joy. It was her grandmother's promise, taking over all her senses. *What once was will be again.*

"We're doing it, Grandma," Carli says. "We're really doing it."

# ABOUT THE AUTHOR

Catherine Weaver is a writer, editor, and educator from the San Francisco Bay Area, where her family has lived for four generations.

She loves gardening, taking walks under the trees, and cuddling up with a good book and her cat.

She is the author of two middle grade fantasy novels and one bilingual English/Japanese picture book.

You can learn more about her at catherineweaverauthor.com.

# A POEM FOR RETIRED LIGHTHOUSES

## Catherine Rockwood

INCREASINGLY abandoned as coastlines alter
and heated waves beat harder rhythms.

Anyone's, for a song
of fighting the tide.

As bridges wash under
as stars blur out of all constellation

my children and their friends draw you:
you, patient light of return
to safe harbours and friendly faces.

*I will always find you* they write to each other
sketching rocks in outline
filling whole skies with colour.

Though old cards and charts speak now
of the gulf, and no known shore,

on page after page in their notebooks
light's spectrum
beams steady to every horizon.

# ABOUT THE AUTHOR

Catherine Rockwood (she/they) lives in Massachusetts with her family. She reads and edits for *Reckoning Magazine*, and reviews books for *Strange Horizons*. Their poetry chapbook, *Endeavors to Obtain Perpetual Motion*, is available from the Ethel Zine Press. A micro-chapbook, *And We Are Far From Shore: Poems for Our Flag Means Death*, is forthcoming from Ethel in 2023.

# THE BOGGART OF CAMPSITE C47

## Holly Schofield

BOGGARTS don't generally pick up rubbish but Moulde has no choice today. Loosening tent pegs, pouring water on sleeping bags, opening cooler lids—nothing discourages this year's campers. Like wild boars across Yorkshire moors, the bloody pillocks just keep marauding through the campgrounds of Alberta Western Provincial Park. What Moulde wouldn't give to be back in the Old Country, back in the olden times when humans weren't such arseholes.

Beyond, down at the slough, the current occupants of campsite C47 are faffing around, throwing rocks at sandpipers and such. Moulde pulls a reeking, empty milk jug out from under a scraggly cedar, a plastic marshmallow bag off struggling bunchberry, and a beer can crushing some long-suffering moss. She fills her cracked leather rucksack with the trash, the one she's been using since 1504. It's got a few centuries left in it, too, because it was crafted with respectful hands, from leather and hemp and magic. Not like today's offensive plastic shite.

When she gets to the campsite, she tips the rubbish out. It makes a right fine pile on the scuffed ground between the camper's shiny minivan and purple nylon tent.

Voices grow louder. With luck, the campers will react to the heap with dismay, and then realize how they're part of the problem. A thick pine next to the picnic table makes a good boggart-sized hiding spot to watch the fun. Moulde crouches on a lower branch, ignoring her rumbling belly. The foothills are scant on edible forage, other than parasite-filled pike or cattail bulbs tasting of sewage. And the campers always bring wrongly coloured food, like hard tiny circles of cereal or that shoe leather they call pizza. What she wouldn't give for a raisin bap or a simple baked potato.

"Holy crap, look! All the crap that we threw away is back here! Gross!" The campers' vocabulary doesn't seem to be any larger than their understanding of how to live a harmonious life. Moulde wants to leap forward and screech, "Ah'll tear ye limb from focking limb, ye dozy bleeders!" but the other boggarts have threatened to cut out her tongue if she does that again. She makes do with a low, disgusted "Pshhh."

The smallest camper, a wee bairn with a fringe of black bangs, stares curiously right at Moulde's pine.

Moulde scuttles away, out the pine's backside and

through tall grasses, then past the raspberry hedge she's planted at the bottom of the scree. She scrambles up the rocky slope on all fours to her cave near the top of the ridge and heads right to the back corner. She huddles there, hands trembling on knobby knees. The world is going to eat itself alive, with all this waste and ruin. Humans have lost their way, lost their very nature, more so than any time she can remember—all of 'em, every last one.

Finally, as dusk threatens, she flicks a finger at the empty oyster shell sitting on the ledge and whispers a few words. The memory of seal oil grows fainter every year but still there's enough magic left to create a faint greenish comforting glow for the next century or two.

A crunch of gravel outside, then: "Found you!" The black-haired girl stares in from the cave entrance. "Hide and seek is my favourite game!"

Moulde screeches and jumps to her feet. "Bloody 'ell! Off wi' ye!"

"You talk funny!"

Moulde studies the girl's bramble-scratched arms, grubby face, and dirty pink overalls. Only one other camper has ever made it this high, a loud posh berk with synthetic clothing. Moulde arranged a "climbing accident" for that one. The campground closed down for a whole peaceful week. Eyes on the girl, she creeps an arm toward the cudgel leaning on the wall.

The girl holds out a fist with something in it. "Wanna share my toast?" Crumbs fall onto the cave floor.

Moulde darts forward, snatches the whole slice, and crams it in her mouth.

"Wow! You must be hungry."

"That I am." Moulde swallows the last bit and clears her throat. "... And I thank ye."

"Karina next door back home says that we are all on one small planet and we have to be nice to each other. So I am!"

Moulde licks butter off her lips. "Does she now?"

"And she says that we are part of the forest and the prairie and the ocean."

"Aye?" Moulde rubs a hairy ear. Was it possible? Could there be a few less daft humans about these days? Her heart feels a warm tinge of long-forgotten pleasure.

"And that we should practice self-care. To the planet, I mean. Because we're part of it."

Moulde sets the cudgel back down. This Karina-next-door-back-home that the bairn is rattling on about sounds like they might have a proper head on their shoulders. And so does the bairn. Such things should be encouraged. Never let it be said that auld Moulde doesn't do her part. She pulls the oyster shell off the shelf and blows out the flame. Shared magic led to increased magic, and that could help the world, p'raps. "Take this home wi' ye, there's a lass."

"Thank you. Um ..." The girl turns it over. "Is it special?"

"Aye. It's got a sense o' the world, it does. A memory, like." Its influence on the bairn would be small and the nights ahead for Moulde blacker than treacle, but it's all she has to give. She makes the flame again and douses it, then has the girl practice until she can do it too. The bairn's enough in harmony with nature that she learns quickly.

"Cool! I gotta go. Mom'll be worried."

"Off wi' ye, then. And, lass—" Moulde gives her the look that makes brownies keel over in a faint. "This chat we've had —it's secret, mind!"

"OK! I like secrets almost as much as forests!"

"Remember today when tha grows auld. Magic be real if ye live in harmony." She squints up at her. "And teach the others? To stop wrecking the forest and the oceans? Will ye?"

"You betcha!" The girl beams and puts the shell in her overall bib pocket. She disappears down the slope in a clatter of pebbles.

Moulde curls up in the dark on her damp cattail mat. Tomorrow, if the next batch of campers have as much in their noggins as this bairn, she'll go easy on them. Just a few wee spiders in their coffee mugs, p'raps—not a whole nest.

# ABOUT THE AUTHOR

Holly Schofield travels through time at the rate of one second per second, oscillating between the alternate realities of city and country life. Her short stories have appeared in *Analog, Lightspeed, Escape Pod,* and many other publications throughout the world. She hopes to save the world through science fiction and homegrown heritage tomatoes. Find her at hollyschofield.wordpress.com.

# REWILDING INDIANA
## Susan Kaye Quinn

I'M Joanna Appleseed, reseeding native gardens from above.

Just a cloud chasing wind, transparent kites to gather the sun, furl them in before the storm. Light as a gull, composites and silk, shift and rise through the layers. The troposphere's a 3D puzzle, navigation by wind on my cheek.

Neutral buoyancy and clean electrons power my days.

I glide near the earth, spotting elk and spraying buckets of seed, taking photos and leaving water footprints in the sky.

The rewilding of Indiana is a thing to see.

Tangled forests and bison herds, thick living coats that hug the land.

Ten million acres back to the wilds before we're done.

Days off, I float.

Or skim cities, dodging solar spires that rise from urban greens so dense, the streets have become myth. My electric carrier pigeons buzz down precious featherweight cargo: vaccines and yarn, spices and seed packets to share. By night,

I talk to satellites and listen to stars, tales of travellers past read by moonlight and the Milky Way.

Trade-wind riders, scientists, seedcroppers like me, we sing sky shanties across the air waves, of wind we didn't catch and girls we didn't kiss.

Watch the downdraft! Shear winds ahoy!

We chatter and stormwatch, weaving stories and invisible safety nets in the sky.

When all is done, grapple ports bring me in safe.

I land long enough to kiss the earth and my love, an earth-bound night of delight.

Then I'm on the wind once more.

# ABOUT THE AUTHOR

Susan Kaye Quinn is an environmental engineer/rocket scientist turned speculative fiction author who now uses her PhD to invent cool stuff in books. Her works range from hopepunk climate fiction to futuristic spec fic, cyberpunk, and steampunk romance. Sue believes being gentle and healing is radical and disruptive. Her short fiction can be found in DreamForge and Grist's Imagine 2200 contest, and her cli-fi novel series (and all her works) can be found on her website: www.susankayequinn.com.

# A LOT FULL OF WEEDS

## T. K. Rex

SOMETIMES, especially days the air was easy to breathe, I liked
to walk all the way down to Golden Gate Park, wander
through the trees, maybe get a taco, watch the waves at
Ocean Beach, or the roller skaters down by Fulton. Maybe
just sit on the playground swings and listen to the birds and
kids. Get reminded there was more to life than my Slack-
infested laptop and my fourth-floor view of a vacant
Tenderloin lot.

The day I got the seeds, Golden Gate Park was bright and
sunny, warm the way it is sometimes in late September, and
the air was golden-brown but the quality a decent 65 that day,
I guess the smoke was too high up to get to us.

I followed the beat of drums to their circle. Fifteen,
maybe twenty people drummed, all sitting in the grass, some
with hand drums, some with big guys held between their
knees. The beats were like the branches of the trees above, I
thought, a branching fractal chaos, a balance between rules

and randomness, self-organizing in the sun.

An ambiguously raced and gendered Gen X burner walked up, nodded, tossed a small brown ball to me from an embroidered, well-loved bag. I caught the ball, and looked at it, confused. The burner winked, said two words—*seed bomb*—and kept walking.

The ball was clay, and speckled, and I didn't really want it, but the burner was long gone. I felt funny throwing it away, so I put it in my pocket and left the drummers to their drums.

Heading back to my apartment in the Tenderloin, I stopped for boba, looked up *seed bomb* on my phone. That led me down a rabbit hole to rewilding and solarpunk and anti-civ, and I looked around at all my houseplants and my little grey-brown cat when I got home, and felt a pang I sometimes do remembering the woods I used to play in as a kid.

I thought often of the empty lot across the street. It'd been empty the entire time I'd lived in San Francisco, just a quarter of a block with fucking nothing on it, blocked off by a chain link fence and filled with weeds, while all my neighbours without homes were sleeping in the nooks and crannies of the sidewalk, the lucky few with tents harassed by dudes who worked at Twitter and believed completely that they got there on their own, that anyone could do the same, if they just worked hard, if they only bothered to learn C++.

I'd worked hard. I'd impressed the right startup at the right time.

But I was not a dude and I had once, when I was seventeen, slept on a friend's sofa for a summer after my dad kicked me out on the sidewalk, a year after his second divorce, screaming at me for being just like every other woman in his life, whatever that meant, and I still remembered my friend's baby, and how his first word was fuck, and how the man she married at eighteen and was divorcing at nineteen kept coming by wasted with threats, and I don't know what ever happened to him, but she and I and the baby all turned out OK. It wasn't a given, though. It was a never a given and the line between close call and tragedy is always just somebody else.

A couple mornings later while the fog was still low and the streets were near their quietest, I walked past the lot full of weeds and I tossed in the little clay ball, hoping no one would see. I worried someone might think I was littering, though the sidewalks were all smeared with shit and a trashcan had thrown up its contents on the next block overnight. I felt I was breaking some kind of law.

It felt kind of good.

And then I felt silly, and walked to the coffee shop but it was too early, so I went home, hugged my cat, and ate almond-milked Raisin Bran, mentally preparing for another day of laptop meetings.

I fell asleep around ten to YouTube explainers on mutual aid, half-heartedly daring the algorithm to radicalize me.

Birds woke me up.

Little song birds, not pigeons or seagulls. They weren't too rare in the city, especially where big, shady trees made cracks in the sidewalk, but I didn't hear them often downtown.

The cat and I looked out the window, and the lot across the street was filled with young trees, just barely taller than the chain link fence containing them.

Someone had gone much further than I in the night. Respect.

The next day a hole appeared in the fence, and the trees seemed a little bigger after people started sleeping underneath them. A week later, the whole fence was down and the cops came around, but didn't seem to give a fuck about the trees or how they got there, they just wanted all the people who'd started camping out between them to go back to the piss-streaked concrete corners they'd been in the week before.

I walked by the lot almost every day, but when the wrecked fence was finally hauled up off the sidewalk it seemed safer, somehow, to go in myself and check it out. There must have been something in the soil there, because the trees were already bigger, fuller than the morning I first saw them. It felt like walking through an orchard, only a little more chaotic, but fruits grew from some of the branches, bright colours speckling the green. A white woman I recognized from my building was filling a canvas bag with avocados she picked up from the leaf litter (how was there leaf litter after only a week?) while her dog waited patiently on its leash. I was sure I remembered her having a shiba, but now it looked more like a mutt, with a long bushy tail.

*These avocados are perfect*, she said when she saw me. *I made guacamole last night with the first two I found and it was so good.*

There were citrus trees, too, and apples and pomegranates. I think some were oaks and walnuts and chestnuts. And the figs grew soft and plump and sweet and I realized I'd just been standing there moving them from the tree to my mouth for ten minutes before a Black guy in jeans and a brown leather jacket walked by with a flute and I smiled at him and offered a fig, and he took it and nodded, played a high note, and pranced on through the trees.

I was late to a meeting when I got back to my laptop. One of the bros in the call was waxing poetic about meritocracy, and I said something sarcastic but I was on mute, just as well, so I sighed and leaned back and admired my bowl of persimmons grown right over there. My cat sniffed at them cutely on the kitchenette counter.

My window was open and through the traffic and yelling and sirens and condo construction on Leavenworth, I could still hear the songbirds.

A week later the forest towered as tall as the buildings that bordered two sides of it. One of the buildings sprang some kind of leak, and water cascaded down the once-muraled brick. At just the right time of day, the sun splashed the water, throwing patterns of light on my kitchenette wall. Algae stained the brick green and ferns grew in the cracks between bricks. Down on the floor of the forest, a pool formed and from there the water made a small stream, under the sidewalk and into the storm drain, presumably out to the Bay. The water was clear and sometimes I saw my street-dwelling neighbours washing their clothes in the pool, bathing under the moon in the glittering leak.

Some of the trees grew wide over time, and by November when rain finally came, there were holes in their trunks the right size for a person to sleep. And as each one appeared, someone moved in. I'd see folks curled up in their holes, reading a book or peeling an orange, cozy with blankets they'd washed in the stream and dried in the sun.

The cops came back sometimes but whenever it looked like they came there to bully the tree dwellers out, they just ended up chatting, and smiling, and pointing out birds. Down the street where the tents were still blocking the boarded-up storefronts, the cops were still dicks, but right here, in the lot, there was something, the smell of the loam, the moss on the trees, that kept them at peace.

I picked up an app, there were so many birds. I spent afternoons looking them up—scrub jays and Steller's, house finches, juncos, red-masked conures, tiny brown wrens, spotted towhees, and even an oriole, bright orange and shy.

One foggy morning, with coffee, I saw a deer through the trees, antlers and all, and he saw me, too. We stared at each other for one frozen moment, then I sipped my coffee and he chewed a twig and we went on with our days.

By the time it was cold—San Francisco cold, like mid-40s —the holes in the widest trees were as big as a tent on the inside and someone had donated makeshift doors to each one, old floral sheets or brown plastic tarps, a beaded curtain or two. Inside at night you could see the soft glow of each denizen's tablet or phone through the beads and the sheets and the leaves and I began to feel jealous, almost, that *I* didn't live in a tree.

By spring the whole corner housed three hundred people, in tree-trunk apartments connected by branches as wide as the sidewalk and burls that spiralled like stairs around trunks, up into the canopy, over the roofs of the rest of the block. It was no-income housing, and a park that grew food, all at the same time, and the people who lived there didn't need money, just tended the forest, kept the trails clear, minded their business like anyone else. I found it hard to imagine they'd once slept on the street—until I went down a few blocks, where nothing had changed.

And I walked past more empty lots every couple of days, and I wondered …

I went back to the drum circle often, hoping to find the old burner, but they never showed up. I even looked up magic seed bombs and GMO trees, and didn't find shit. I asked someone at work if he'd heard of anything like it, and his only reply was a recommendation for naming the place *Airtreentree*.

I began to assume the whole thing was a fluke. It made it more special, somehow, but sad, too. Every lot I walked by was depressing before, but now I saw what it *could be*. If only.

• • •

One day I heard reggae down in the forest and decided to finish my work in the shade. I followed the sound to the stream, and spotted my neighbour with her shiba-turned-grey-fox, kneeling next to a boom box, hands in the mud, with a few other people who lived in the trees. Children splashed in the water and laughed just downstream. My neighbour waved me toward her, and I knelt on her blanket and opened my backpack to pull out my laptop.

It wasn't inside. It was still on my desk. Maybe I should've gone back, but instead I breathed in the scent of the stream and looked up at the sun-backlit leaves.

*What are you up to?*

*Take a handful of clay*, she grinned, *mix it with these.*

A woman with skin like the shade of an oak, who I'd once seen shooting up down on Jones Street, passed me a bowl full of seeds. I smiled and she smiled back and some of her teeth were still gone but she looked so content and well-hydrated now. I realized I knew nothing about her even though I'd walked past her hundreds of times, so I said, *I'm Magenta.* She said, *Call me Jan*, and I took a handful of seeds and mixed them with clay from the ground by the stream, and rolled them around in my palms. Little brown globes, little worlds in waiting. Each one a child of hundreds of trees, a forest that once was a lot full of weeds.

# ABOUT THE AUTHOR

T. K. Rex (she/they) is a science fiction and fantasy author whose stories have appeared in *Asimov's*, *Gizmodo*, *Reckoning*, and many other places. She's a member of the Science Fiction & Fantasy Writers Association, the Writers Grotto, and the infamous Clarion Ghost Class of 2020/21/22. T. K. grew up in Northern California and New Mexico with Wiccan parents of mostly British and Ashkenazi descent, and spends her free time gaming, hiking around the Bay Area, and photographing street art in her San Francisco neighbourhood, where she lives with her artist/musician partner and their two enormous tuxedo cats.

# 120° IN THE SHADE

## Susan Lee Simpson

IT'S summer in the southwest
    when talk about the changing weather gets hot
    when resistance weakens and drought-spiked
        fevers linger longer and longer
    when surface water shimmers
        reflect our own empty promises
    when even Russian thistle give up
        their bony hold, tossing skeletons into the wind
    when temperatures bring a rain of feathers and spark wildfires
best to see those flames for what they are: consequences of us
making light of it

# ABOUT THE AUTHOR

Susan Lee Simpson is an emerging BIPOC poet and collage artist seeking to create connections through the written, visual, and book arts. After leaving a 30 year prepandemic career in research/statistical consulting, she is enjoying a new chapter of life, full of right-brain awakening. She lives and creates in Chapel Hill, NC.

# SEEDS, TEMPORARILY IN THEIR BED OF LINT

## Jordan Hirsch

THE puckering taste of lemon lingers in my memory. Bright, like the stars out my window. Distant for now, like them, too.

Eight worlds. Eight worlds in nine standard years. But none of them perfect.

Each star system has plenty of planets orbiting within, swirling in their gravity pools. Most of those are uninhabitable. My scans have shown me that, so I've flown on by.

Eight, though. I've stopped at eight, put down landing struts after a slowing burn through atmospheres with acceptable ranges of nitrogen, oxygen, and so on. I've taken samples, run tests, even dug a hole once.

One hole.

I couldn't bring myself to do it, though. The numbers

were close but not enough. I packed up and went home.

Home used to be a bright yellow pie, tart curd between crumbling crust and marshmallow-y meringue. He'd worry every time, glasses fogging as he'd open the oven door, that it hadn't set properly. Holding his breath as the knife would drop through, the piece holding its shape perfectly from server to plate. Home was that first bite, bringing my tongue alive.

The alert chime brings me back to my cockpit, alone and sleeping sitting up. I haven't used my bed in weeks. I'm entering a new star system, this one with a ninth planet fitting parameters, and I slow the ship, hand resting on the three lumps in my pocket.

Blue with water and promise, there's a place to land between ice-capped mountains and the rolling desert dunes. The air mix is good, and I leave my dusty helmet in its locker —there's no point in stopping at places I need it.

It's the same one I had before leaving; he had a matching one, too, and he wore his more faithfully than I did, the air irritating his deep cedar eyes as waters rose some places and other lush landscapes dried to bone. A doctor gave him eye drops; they only helped a little as we waited for word, moving up the relocation roster.

The foliage on this ninth planet is shades of green I recognize. A lemon tree's chlorophyll won't be too alien here. I test the nearby water, running cool and clear: pH, salinity, ion levels—all acceptable.

We'd been promised families would be called together.

When I was called to pack my bags and he wasn't, we didn't know who to contact. Hours spent on hold only to not have our questions answered, to be transferred to someone else, to have to wait again, and finally, finally, someone guessed it was an error in the system. Our IDs hadn't been linked in the lottery. We'd had two choices.

Patting my pocket, I begin to dig. The soil's rich brown colour is full of death-become-life, full of potential. With everything else growing here, these seeds have a chance. Don't they?

I could've stayed. I could've stayed with him and waited or gone with my call. He'd told me to go, but I shouldn't have listened. He'd told me he'd get called soon and to wait for him where it was safe, where I could breathe, where there was a future.

I shouldn't have listened.

Rock. The steel of my shovel hits rock again and again and again. Dripping sweat, I throw my shovel to the ground. How does anything grow here when the soil's so thin? When it's completely solid underneath?

He came to the station to see me off, kissing my forehead, hugging me one last time over and over. His last words weren't, "I love you." He took my hand, pressing three tiny bumps into them. "Plant them, Ona," he said. "The sooner they're in the ground on our new home, the sooner we'll have lemons for pie."

I start to pack up my things. This isn't it. I can't plant the seeds here.

Carriers left our home, none of them carrying Marcus. I'm sure they were full of great people. We tried to send messages, tried to check in, but the comms were overloaded. Too many people trying to connect with loved ones and friends—others whose IDs hadn't been linked.

Marcus died before there was a carrier for him.

Nearly all my equipment is back on board when I hear a voice.

"Hello, traveller." I turn and see someone, hair long and braided. They've spoken in the pidgin language of Earth's refugees. It's not their native tongue. It's not mine either.

"I'm Atine," they say, and I tell them my name. "What are you doing here?"

"Leaving," I say. My back is to them, and my cheeks are hot as I load the last of my supplies.

"So soon?" they ask, and I don't answer. "Would you like some food for your journey?"

The tart thought of citrus fills my mouth with saliva. It's been so long since I've had something other than rations.

My stomach has its say, and I turn back to them, nodding. Atine rifles in their bag, then pulls out a small loaf of bread. They tear it in two, handing me half.

The yeasty warmth overtakes me like a nightmare, encompassing and haunting. As I chew, crust cracking between my teeth, Atine looks at what I've done—we're surrounded by dozens of filled-in holes.

They nod, as if they know.

"What were you hoping to plant?" Atine asks, and bread

sticks to my tongue.

Marcus had pressed the lemon seeds into my hand, and they'd stayed in my pocket for weeks as the crowded carrier took me farther and farther from him. Away from our trees. Away from our porch swing. Away from the pie plate my mother had given me before she died.

This place I am now, this ninth planet with its mountains, rivers, and shaded meadows of clover-like growth: this could have been our home.

I swallow hard. "A lemon grove," I say, and Atine nods again.

"For whom?" they ask.

It was nearly a year before I got confirmation that he hadn't made it. A friend knew someone in Records; they got me word. I haven't heard someone say his name since. I haven't said it either.

"Marcus." It's barely more than a whisper.

"Marcus," Atine echoes.

We stand together in silence, the bread heavy in my stomach, birds lazing overhead in the sun.

"A lemon grove, hm?" Atine finally says. "My village is close. We have many gardens. We could help you, if you'd like."

The seeds are heavy in my pocket. I've been searching for so long; I only have three.

"You don't have to decide right away," Atine says. "But you're welcome to stay awhile. Eat with us. Rest. Spend some time in the fresh air." They laugh gently, eyeing my pod.

Following Atine to their village, we pass fields of grain, sprawling berry bushes, and vines heavy with grapes.

It was just like we'd talked, Marcus and me.

I don't have to decide now. This could just be a layover for me on the way to planet ten. But the seeds: they are warm in my pocket, as if they know something, and it has me wondering.

If Atine's village can grow here on this ninth planet, why can't I?

# ABOUT THE AUTHOR

Jordan Hirsch writes speculative fiction and poetry in Saint Paul, MN, USA, where she lives with her husband and their two perfect cats. Her work has appeared with *Apparition Literary Magazine*, *Daily Science Fiction*, and other venues.

# MARTIAN BLUE
## Keira Reynolds

"I could have had it all once, you know," she said, between sips of Martian Blue. "The big house back on Mars, the private shuttle, luxury apartments on Titan and Europa, all of it, the whole package. I could have been living the dream."

I laughed, took a big swig of Enceladusian Red, and wiped the foam from my lips with the back of my hand.

"You too, huh?"

Every old prospector has a "one that got away" story.

She looked over her shoulder, leaned over the scratched plastic bar table, and looked me in the eye.

"No. I mean it."

I stopped laughing. I'd known her long enough to know when she was being serious. I also knew that she'd been everywhere and seen everything. I'd been her teacher once, but that was a long time ago. She'd been places and seen things I never had. If she had a story to tell, I wanted to hear it.

"Go on."

"I was on a long-haul prospecting trip. Don't ask me where because I won't tell you. Somewhere way off the beaten track, far from any colonies or shipping routes. Long-range analysis indicated that a planet orbiting one of the stars in the cluster might be capable of supporting life."

"I remember when that was a big deal."

"Yeah, me too, but no one gets excited about alien life anymore, unless it's advanced, and there was no indication of that. There's always the possibility of interesting pharmaceuticals, of course, but mostly I was looking for rare metals. Osdium, ruthidium, irenium, that sort of thing. You know the drill."

I nodded.

"Well, there was life all right," she said. "The place was lush with it. It was all blue and green and white, oceans, forests, mountains, clouds. Reminded me of old images of Earth, back before we screwed everything up."

She stared out of the nearest viewport for a moment, her eyes distant, and took another sip of Martian Blue before she went on.

"I've been around, you know? I've seen a lot. Dust clouds lit by the fires of dying stars, auroras on a dozen planets, sunset on Atropos and moonrise on Nausicaa. Things most people never get to see. But I've never seen anything that moved me the way my first sight of that planet moved me. Even before I landed, just looking at the place from orbit through the viewports, it called to me. Like coming home.

Not that I ever really had a home, but it felt like I imagine coming home must feel, you know? When I close my eyes, I can still see those mountains, hear the wind in the trees, smell the perfume in the air—"

"Wait, what? You breathed the atmosphere?"

"Keep your voice down."

She looked over her shoulder again, checking that my exclamation hadn't drawn any unwanted attention, while I shook my head in disbelief.

"You know better than that," I said. "It takes months, sometimes years, of testing before you can be sure that it's safe to breathe a planet's atmosphere. It doesn't matter how human-friendly the gas mix might be, all it takes is one bacterium or virus to which you have no immunity, and the next thing you know you're convulsing and bleeding from every orifice, and so is everyone who's been in contact with you. How long ago was this?"

"Relax. I'm not patient zero. It was twenty years ago."

"OK. You got lucky. But why?"

"Let me tell my story, and you'll find out."

I waved over a robot waiter and ordered another Martian Blue for her and another Enceladusian Red for me. She waited until the robot left before she continued.

"I landed in a clearing in a forest in the northern temperate zone and sent out drones. The drones were barely out of the hatches when they started reporting lorintium."

"You found lorintium? Stars! You weren't kidding. You hit the jackpot. Was there much of it?"

"That's the thing. I thought at first the drones had to be wrong. There couldn't be that much lorintium on one planet. If what the drones were reporting was correct, there was more lorintium on that one planet than had ever been found before on all the explored planets put together."

"That's impossible."

"That's what I thought. So, I decided to get a closer look. The drones were finding plenty of animal life out there, but nothing that appeared dangerous, not to an experienced prospector in an armoured suit. So, I suited up, grabbed a prospecting kit, and went out to see for myself. And it was true. The stuff was everywhere. I didn't even have to dig for it. The rocks were full of lorintium. And it wasn't just a small local outcrop. I walked for a kilometre, and I sent out drones over a hundred kilometres, and everywhere it was the same. There was lorintium, lots of it, everywhere."

"So, what went wrong? How come you're sitting here talking to me instead of … I dunno. I can't even imagine what you could do with all the credits you'd get for finding that much lorintium."

The robot waiter came back with our drinks. I scanned my wrist implant to pay for them, and again she waited until the robot left before she continued. Robot waiters aren't supposed to record audio, but there are rumours sometimes. She wasn't taking any chances.

"I'd seen enough to convince myself that there was no mistake. There really was that much lorintium. I was about to return to the lander and call it in, when I saw the fairies."

I choked on a mouthful of Enceladusian Red.

"*Fairies?* Has this whole thing been a windup?"

She shook her head.

"That's just what I call them, for want of a better name. I'm not saying they were really fairies, like in the old stories, any more than the 'trees' were really trees. I'm not saying they were magic or supernatural, or anything. Except … well, hear me out, and you can decide for yourself. They were humanoid, they were about ten centimetres tall, and they had wings, like butterfly wings, covered in shining, iridescent scales. Stars! They were beautiful. The colours of their wings reminded me of auroras on Dinesha, or the crystal fields on Raiden, when the light hits them just right, or rainbows on Vulcanus. But honestly, none of those comparisons really comes close. And their voices! I heard an old recording once, of a lark singing back on Earth. Their voices were like that. It was they who told me it was safe to breathe the air."

"You understood them? How?"

"I don't know. That's the thing I can't explain. I don't know how I understood them, but I did, and they understood me. They sang to me, and told me stories, and I understood it all. I took off my suit and walked with them barefoot in the grass. I ate the fruit they gave me and drank the water they brought in shells from a nearby stream."

I shuddered at the thought.

"Do you know how many horror movies start like that?"

"They told me it was safe."

"How could they know what was safe for you? And how

could you be sure they were telling the truth? Assuring the giant alien that it's safe to eat the big blue berries could be a very convenient way to get rid of an invader when you're ten centimetres tall."

"I didn't just understand their words. I understood their thoughts and their feelings, and they understood mine. I don't think they're capable of lying. I don't think they know what lying is."

"OK. I mean, I can't pretend to understand, not really. Sounds like hypnotism to me, but here you are, alive and well, so I dunno. Go on. What happened next?"

"I thought about what would happen when the Company came for the lorintium. I thought about bulldozers ripping up the forest, and about drills and crushers tearing up the earth. I thought about mining waste poisoning the air, and the soil, and the water. They felt what I was feeling, saw what I was seeing, and I felt their fear, their pain, their horror, and their incomprehension. I saw us through their eyes, and in their eyes, we were monsters."

"What did you do?"

"I went back to the ship. I sat there, staring at the comms console for the longest time. Then I wiped every hint of lorintium from the data and called it in NOI."

"Nothing of interest? The largest deposit ever found, of the most valuable resource in the universe, and you reported nothing of interest?"

"Yes. I had to. I couldn't be that monster."

I sat back and took a long swig of Enceladusian Red

while I wondered what I would have done in her place.

"Did you ever go back?"

"No, and I never will. Someone might wonder what I was doing way out there and decide to investigate."

Her wrist implant vibrated. She knocked back the last of her Martian Blue and stood up, slinging her backpack over one shoulder.

"That's my flight. Time to go. See you around."

I stood up. We shook hands and hugged. We both knew that, given our nomadic lifestyles, there was a good chance that every time we parted might be the last. But we never talked about that.

"I can trust you with this, can't I?" She looked me in the eye.

She pulled me out of a tar pit on Aurigae, dug me out from under a rockslide on Beta Pictoris, and had my back in more bar fights than I could remember. I would have died for her ten times over. But I wasn't about to tell her that.

"You can trust me. But you know there's no guarantee someone won't find that place someday. You gave up unimaginable riches, a life of luxury and security, and it could all be for nothing."

"It's a very remote cluster. It's very expensive to send someone out there. There's no reason for the Company to send anyone out that way again now that it's been declared NOI."

"But it's not impossible. It could happen."

"It could." She smiled at me over her shoulder as she

turned to leave. "But if it does, it won't happen because of me."

## ABOUT THE AUTHOR

Keira Reynolds is a trans woman, a software developer turned writer. She is currently studying Arts and Humanities, with a specialisation in Creative Writing, with the Open University. She lives with her wife Julie in County Kerry, Ireland. She loves Ireland, but not the Irish weather, and dreams of escaping to somewhere warm and sunny. She occasionally posts random thoughts on her blog at keirareynolds.com.

# RETURNAL
## Ben Lockwood

It's March again, and with the drizzling grey comes the thirty-fifth anniversary of the return of our vessel, the *Pursuant*. I've grown old in the years since, and as I gaze out my window at a world caught between the death of winter and the renewal of spring, it feels important to write down some words about what happened, while I still remember them. Although I have nothing new to say about the mission that has not already been said, I pray this time it finds purchase.

*Mission.* The word seems insufficient for the gravity of what we sought. It was planned on the advent of a new technology; one that transformed the fabric of space, bringing distances closer to us as we travelled toward them. Describing the mechanics of it now would be ironic, given the disbelief we were met with upon our return. Suffice it to say that it was a hallowed discovery that sobered humanity, focusing us toward a collective search of the heavens.

In eight years, we built the ship and the drive that powered it. It's hard to overstate what a colossal achievement this was amid the turmoil of that time. Bloodshed and devastation raged everywhere, on scales never before possible. Then, a miracle of engineering emerged. We were suddenly met with the ability to seek answers in the cosmos. It was as if, while drowning in our self-annihilation, a lifeline had appeared ready to pull us into a new era of civilization. We devoted everything to its manifestation.

The clarity was short-lived, though. In the months that led to our launch, old conflicts erupted among the various capitalists and imperialists involved. Nations committed acts of unimaginable violence against each other as they unleashed new engines of destruction in what came to be known as The War of Discovery. By the time of our launch date, the fighting had killed twenty million people.

On the eve of our undertaking, our commanding assembly—a chosen group of representatives from what was formerly the United Nations—charged us with a single directive: find consciousness amongst the stars and seek their counsel. If this was surprising, it was only because of what was left unsaid. No planet, habitable or not, could save us from ourselves.

It took us a month to reach the edge of the solar system, where we were scheduled to turn on the drive and leave behind any possibility of communication with the rest of humanity. Many of us turned to religion to deal with the coming trauma. Ceremonies of Buddhist, Christian, Jewish, Muslim, and other orders became increasingly common until we finally reached our send-off destination, where we received one final transmission from Earth: *Fly home to new worlds.*

Once into the breach of space our collective anxiety seemed to ease, and we took to our mission with an almost fanatic zeal. We were driven by a holy, universal quest to find a cosmic saviour.

We began our search with the worlds that scientists had deemed most likely to contain life. We scoured solar systems with multiple planets, some with multiple stars, and even some with no stars. And although we found only empty, lifeless places, our optimism remained high for some time.

Two years into our four-year mission we approached another threshold. The nature of our drive distorted our experience of time such that after this point it became virtually certain that anyone we had known on Earth had now passed. Our pace, and the laws of probability, predicted another five years of searching in order to reach the number of worlds required to statistically guarantee finding intelligent life. If any existed.

So, we went on. Pushing past the vision of humanity's greatest lenses and into the absolute unknown.

We found nothing in the oblivion that followed, and it wasn't long before the darkness of deep space found its way inside. Paranoia, and eventually madness, spread through us like a disease. The resulting infights nearly ruined us. When the violence finally ceased, two-thirds of the crew were lost. Seventy-two lights of humanity extinguished into the void.

The survivors vowed to hold true to our goal, though we came to know a somber kind of harmony in each other. It bound us together through what was ultimately a fifteen-year mission; eleven more than had been originally planned.

In the end we found nothing: no intelligence, no consciousness, no life at all. The despair of this was immense, as incomprehensibly large as the universe itself. Twelve of our remaining forty crew members jettisoned themselves out the airlocks and into the abyss.

The few of us that remained saw no choice but to return home. The trip would take us another year and a half, extending our total time away to three hundred and forty-two years on Earth. We set a course, though we did not know what, if anything, would be waiting for us.

Returning to Earth, we found a solar system teeming with signs of life. Probes, satellites, and even shipping cargos buzzed between planets. Technological advances had granted humanity the means to extend its boundaries, though it seemed to have lost the kind of engineering that had sent us to the stars.

Various sensors alerted the world to our presence much sooner than we anticipated. We scrambled to send a message, but the temporal gulf between our machines was too great. We were fired upon by interplanetary batteries before we could identify ourselves. The attack decimated our ship, killing nineteen members of our remaining crew.

The history of the subsequent events has occurred within living memory but is worth repeating. The nine surviving members of *The Pursuant* were captured after our blazing crash into Earth's atmosphere sent pieces of our interstellar home streaking across the skies of both hemispheres. We were branded immediately as heretics for telling our story to a world that had forgotten us; we were interrogated, imprisoned, tortured, and ultimately—when no satisfactory answers to the mystery of our appearance could be ascertained—released into exile.

In the decade that followed, several of us were assassinated after attempting to refute the occultist fantasies that originated upon our return. Acolytes raised altars around sites of wreckage from our ship and prayed to the cosmic deities they imagined had cast us out.

It wasn't long before the scientists and engineers of this new era began collecting pieces of our ship to reconstruct the technology they had lost. In the last decade, they have apparently made great strides in this effort, and now the leaders of our world announce that humanity will soon embark upon a new voyage into the stars, to find the life they claim we have hidden from them.

For this reason, I have emerged from my exile to herald a warning, as the sole living member of that mission. There is nothing waiting for us in the empty vastness of space. There is no great and wise consciousness to which we can turn for answers to the questions that haunt us. There are no beings that can help us escape our own destruction.

The life we seek in the cosmos is here.

## ABOUT THE AUTHOR

Ben Lockwood is an ecologist at Penn State University. He's also a socialist, unionist, and prison abolitionist. Ben's fiction appears (or is forthcoming) in *Tree and Stone Magazine*, *Creepy Podcast*, Black Hare Press, *Metastellar*, and others. You can find Ben wasting time on Twitter and Instagram (@brlockwood), and on Mastodon (benlockwood@fediscience.org).

# VENI VIDI VICI

## Patrick Johnson

WHEN we rose from the stasis of our species' sleep,
She was our terror: nighttime noise, suspicious breeze.

When we wrangled the land into neat plots and squares,
She was our burden: cold, ruin, hunger, disease.

When we harnessed her blood, black, and her bones, black too,
She was our spoils: oil rigs, smokestacks, slick factories.

Now, we bore of survival and set fires for sport,
Orphaning ourselves, swallowing the rising seas.

# ABOUT THE AUTHOR

Patrick Johnson is an emerging, Queer poet from Queens, New York. He is a public school science teacher and labor union advocate. His poetry draws from many themes, often inspired by human history, loss, and family. He facilitates a biweekly poetry workshop, and enjoys supporting other poets in their artistic journeys.

# SING THE PHOENIX TO FLAME

## Jenna Hanchey

ONCE, Tena Na Tena had been certain when she sang. Injustice gathered within her, swirling tighter until it solidified into a beat, lyrics, melody. When it clicked into place, she let it out. It wasn't as if she planned carefully, weighing the implications of her words or the mode of release. She knew right and she knew wrong. And when the Interplanetary Trade Authority denied formal recognition to the Pan-African Alliance in their negotiations with the Mars delegation, it was wrong. So she sang. That was all there was to it.

Now, another song stretched up from the chaos within her. She pulled it back, mental gravity making escape velocity impossible. She'd lost everything last time—accounts, access, even the life of a friend in the fallout. Everything, except

Furaha. And for Furaha's sake, she couldn't do it again.

"*Eti*, Tena? You ready?" Furaha adjusted her tight-fitting *kitenge* dress, smoothing the fabric over her hips.

Tena lifted her eyebrows slightly in assent. "Only let me fix my headwrap, then *twende*."

"OK, dear, I can go to the lobby to call a taxi."

"I am coming."

Headwrap done, Tena remained seated on the hotel bed in an unflattering black dress, staring at the mirror. The idea of going to the ITA gala tonight sent frost seeping out from her heart, until she felt as immobile as an iceberg. Able to do nothing but drift where the frigid seas of fate willed.

Visions of the frozen blocks danced in her mind, holding tender memories within their rigid restrictions. Ice wasn't something people wasted energy making *kijijini*. Before moving to Dar es Salaam, Tena had rarely seen it. But in the city people made useless things in order to impress. And after three dates, Furaha had wanted to impress her. She'd known Furaha's work in the Tanzanian representative's office paid well, but she hadn't really understood until soaring up in the elevator that night. When the doors opened and she stepped into the rotating restaurant overlooking Dar es Salaam, Tena felt high and strong as Kilimanjaro itself. Only glass separated her from the vast world spread out below. She occupied the far reaches of air, where even water stopped flowing, frozen into its crystalline form. She hadn't understood enough to be frightened of those reaches yet.

One hand linked across the table with Furaha's, Tena had

swirled the translucent squares in her glass. Watching them dance. Entranced by their tragic tale. Water, once boiling over with joy, ferociously ridding itself of contaminants, only to then be forced into a box and trapped there. Frozen.

Tena had wondered then how long it would take to melt again. To be free. She wondered again now.

She couldn't feel her toes in her new shoes. But Furaha told her they were perfect—restrained, remorseful. Since the ITA had stripped her data from every internationally recognized cyber system, she did what Furaha told her to do. Even if that meant wearing these stupid heels and putting on the performance of a lifetime. Swallowing her rage and smiling at the gala.

Furaha was no fool. She understood why this was hard for Tena, to attend a celebration of opulence while her people struggled to eat. Consorting with those who stripped her community's resources and replaced them with toxic waste. Those whom she sang against, all those years ago, when they tried to prevent the Pan-African Alliance from trading their solar-powered machinery with the Martian colonists. Who decimated her life. Furaha understood, but she didn't feel it. Instead, she calculated. Scouring for opportunities, taking losses in stride, focusing on the long term. She was strong. Stronger than Tena. Able to work inside the system without burning out.

Furaha had laboured for years on her plan: phased infiltration of the ITA with international webs of saboteurs leading to a multipronged coordinated cyberattack. And tonight, part of that labour was rehabilitating Tena's image to bring her into the fold. Cementing the impression that Tena was no longer threatening, but a cautionary tale. The radical brought to heel at the feet of power. The reasoning was sound. And it was only a small sacrifice, really, to go the gala tonight.

Even if it hardened her once boiling soul into a compact cube of shame.

Sucking her teeth, Tena turned away from the blank gaze reflected in the mirror and swept out of the room.

Like many things in New York, the elevator felt excessive. Glazed glass and silver filigree, complete with an operator to ensure passengers literally needn't lift a finger. God forbid their hands graze anything touched by those less desirable. Tena was under no illusions as to who was considered less desirable here.

She greeted the operator. Poor man, in his ridiculous suit. "How are you, sir?"

"Just fine, ma'am." He nodded over his shoulder to be polite. Eyes widening, he turned around. "No way. You're Tena Na Tena!"

"True," she acknowledged.

"Is it also true what you sang? That your mother named you Tena because—"

"*Tena na tena* we must rise up, 'cuz again and again they force us to fall, make us crawl, take it all. Tell us to be grateful," she lightly rapped. And tensed, reflexively.

His warm grin loosened the ice beneath her skin, the

structure that had been holding this made-up version of her together. Tentatively, she wiggled her toes, testing the shoes' limits. She could see now that the face under the operator's hat was younger than she expected, and only a few shades lighter than her own.

"You must have been a child when I last sang," she clucked.

"I was! I grew up with your music! I'm Peter. Mama Angie, that's my grandma, she used to tell us about the day you sang outside the ITA meeting in Switzerland. She was watching the original vidstream, even before it cut out and everyone else took up filming." Horror flashed across his face. "I mean, I'm so sorry about your friend. He was doing a good thing, he—"

"He did not deserve that death."

"No, he didn't. And you didn't deserve any of that shit they did to you either. But damn, you got them scrambling. They *had* to recognize the Pan-African Alliance after that! Even with the restrictions they eventually slammed down, I tell you what, it gave us a lot of strength knowing those stories." He paused. "You doing OK, though?"

"I am … doing what I have to."

"I feel that," he said, grimacing at his operator's outfit.

"Exactly," she commiserated, gesturing at her own bland black gown.

In the ensuing pause, Tena felt herself stiffen with each floor the elevator dropped.

"Oh hey!" Peter interrupted before the weight of silence

could crush her. He rustled in his pocket, pulling out a small flyer folded in half. She raised an eyebrow. Paper was unusual in these days of digital domination.

As she took it, he explained, "It's sort of embarrassing, but, uh, you're kinda an inspiration for us. We have a weekly meeting named after you. *Tena Na Tena.* We mostly keep it analog, you get why. But we're looking into this Zimbabwean platform that has some pretty wild features! Gets around restricted neuralink access, for one. It's even rumoured they're training anticolonial AI to protect servers from ITA interference …"

Tena gently unfolded the flyer, Peter's words turning to a buzz. *Tena Na Tena: Queens Branch #5,* the heading read. Underneath was an ink drawing. Wings of flame spread high, encircling a head that resembled both bird and woman, topped with kitenge patterning. The same pattern intertwined with the feathery flames below, making the figure's gown look both undeniably African and woven from fire. The image was only ink on paper, but it seemed to move as Tena stared at it, mingling until bird became indistinguishable from woman, clothing from embodiment.

Everything ablaze.

"… the potential, right? A coordinated interruption of ITA systems!"

She felt a crack inside her as a song leapt fully formed from her mind, melting through her defenses. Water, liquid once more, filled her eyes. She must have looked wild, because Peter quickly added, "Don't worry, camera up there's a dummy. The wealthy-ass folks as stay here pay to not get caught. We're completely off-the-record."

The elevator stopped abruptly, knocking her off-balance. She almost twisted her ankle—these damn shoes!—but recovered quickly, backing into the corner as a pale man in a fitted suit stepped into the enclosed space.

They rode quietly. Peter faced forward once again. Tena stared at the paper in her hand. She kept it carefully hidden from the other passenger's sight, even though the hand lifted to his temple indicated he was scrolling through a neuralink interface. Tena had never bothered to get one, after her data had been blasted from cyberspace. After her last song had burned down her life, leaving her unable to lift herself from the ashes.

Wait, had Peter been saying—

With a soft ding, the elevator opened on the lobby. The other passenger quickly strode away. But Tena didn't move. She spied Furaha across the crowd of people, bright colour in a sea of grey. The only light in a vast darkness. She wished she were the type of strong that Furaha needed. A woman who could stand with her, undermining the system from within, facing injustice every day without yielding. Biting down her rage, holding the flames behind an impenetrable shield of ice.

The heavy metal door slid shut.

Peter shot her a glance. Reaching over him, Tena pushed the button for the top floor.

Her strength was not in persistence. It was in explosion.

"Tell me more about this platform out of Zimbabwe." She yanked the restrictive shoes off her feet, stretching her toes wide. "And do you have any more of that paper? I have an idea for a song."

## ABOUT THE AUTHOR

Jenna Hanchey has been an actress, particle physicist, Peace Corps volunteer, and afterschool-space-program teacher. She is currently a professor of critical/cultural studies whose research looks at how speculative fiction can imagine decolonization and bring it into being. Her own writing tries to support this project of creating better futures for us all. Her stories appear in *Nature: Futures*, *Daily Science Fiction*, *Medusa Tales*, *Wyngraf*, and *Martian Magazine*, among other venues. Having once been called a "badass fairy," she attempts to live up to the title. Follow her adventures on Twitter (@jennahanchey) or at www.jennahanchey.com.

# THE SAND SHIP BUILDERS OF CHITUNGWIZA

## Masimba Musodza

THE sound of the men and women working outside snatched him from that surreal world between a dream and reality. Muchenjeri could not sit up unaided; the last time he had been able to do that, he reflected, everything else in his world worked too. Ten years ago.

He had been on a visit to Zimbabwe, the land of his birth, when the government finally responded to the Covid-19 outbreak and announced a lockdown and travel ban. By the time it was lifted, race riots broke out all over the United Kingdom in response to an incident of police brutality in the United States. Then came the terror attacks and total war in the Middle East and Afghanistan as the United States withdrew its troops. North Korea collapsed. China collapsed. The United States collapsed, divided among its traditional conservative and progressive factions, and a small but belligerent white nationalist entity.

Zimbabwe was already on the brink before any of this started. Muchenjeri recalled that he could still use his legs when the telecommunications system went. It was the week that the electricity went for good that he had the car accident that left him paralyzed from the waist down.

The aroma of baobab porridge wafted into his musings as a shadow fell over the cave. Chiga came in, and knelt before him, placing the bowl on the floor. She planted a kiss on his forehead. "Good morning, my love."

As she helped him sit up, she said, "One of the scouts reports that Marauders are headed this way. I thought they had all gone north. I thought that is why we have been safe here!"

"Your brother thought all the Marauders had gone north," said Muchenjeri. "But I knew that it was only a matter of time before our activities attracted attention."

"Six people have been expelled from here," said Chiga, thoughtfully. "So many people with a grudge." She sat beside him, leaning against the wall of the cave, and began to feed him. Later, she would inspect her desert reclamation project along what used to be the Manyame River.

A shadow fell across the cave again, and Munaku burst in, crouching before his mother and stepfather. *"Baba,* the chief requests your presence at an extraordinary session of the

Council!"

"As my lord wishes," said Muchenjeri.

The teenager nodded respectfully and departed. Muchenjeri loved the boy dearly. He was everything a man could hope for in a son. He had shown an aptitude and initiative for Muchenjeri's mission to preserve technology and knowledge for the survival of the people. Munaku had organized an expedition to the schools of the abandoned city of Chitungwiza and collected calculators. Their scavenged solar panels now powered some of the lights in the caves.

About three-quarters of an hour later, Chiga wheeled her husband to the Chief's Courtyard. They traversed a bleak landscape of brown, cracked earth, punctuated by the odd resilient tree to the old school buildings that Chief Seke Mutema III had claimed as his government seat. The hot, dry air seared Muchenjeri's throat. He reached for the plastic tubing that linked with the plastic bottle strapped to the back of his wheelchair and sipped gratefully. Water seeped through the granite of the caves and collected in pools.

Behind this cluster of buildings, nearly on the horizon, the abandoned city of Chitungwiza rose against the blue sky. As the couple circumnavigated the buildings, the shacks that housed most of the five hundred residents of this settlement sailed into view. As did the sand ships.

It had been a full week since Muchenjeri had left the caves among the *dwalas* where the Technocrats, all ten of them, lived. The progress made on the three main sand ships staggered him. They were lined up on what would have been the sports ground. Salvaged from long-distance haulage trucks and buses, with masts made from streetlamps, they resembled giant works of metal sculpture. Each of them could accommodate about a hundred people. There were fifteen smaller vehicles, prototypes, to meet the shortfall, but there were enough to move the entire Chiefdom of Seke Mutema III.

The wind blew, lifting a wave of dust that floated like a ghost across the waste before dissipating. A sizable crowd had already gathered in the school courtyard. This is where assembly would have been held. Muchenjeri's mind wandered to the time he stood in such a courtyard, a gangly, clean-shaven lad in a uniform several sizes too big, one his parents expected him to grow into. The time before the global catastrophe. The time before the national catastrophe that had sent millions into exile. The time when the people knew not calamity and despondency, but the exuberance of postcolonial optimism. When the land was green and the rain came in due season.

A hushed tone descended on the crowd, as Muchenjeri and Chiga, each a distinguished technical expert and member of the council, proceeded to the steps, an improvised dais where sat with almost theatrical aplomb Chief Seke Mutema III and his officials and wives. Like Muchenjeri, the former Brian Manyame had been visiting Zimbabwe from a foreign base when Covid-19 broke out. After nearly a million people had abandoned the city of Chitungwiza, he had led this group to the wastelands on the periphery. Six years later, they had managed to not only survive the harsh climate and the collapse of civilization, but had begun to thrive.

It was this progression from merely trying to stay alive, reverting to skills and a social order that had not been needed for over a century and a half, to beginning to find purpose and beauty in life that allowed a new centre of power to begin to rise in the community to challenge that of the chief. Muchenjeri and Chiga, the chief's sister, had worked assiduously to archive knowledge on recovered external hard drives. They had organized studies to understand the radically transformed ecology and meteorology, and to inventory surviving flora and fauna that could be cultivated to sustain life. They had maintained a school and encouraged youth creativity and initiative. It was becoming increasingly apparent that their vision offered a more secure and sustainable future than the regimental tribal regime of Chief Seke Mutema III, which could be regarded as merely a more refined form of the Marauder bands.

As Munaku placed his stepfather's wheelchair near the chief and kicked the brake down with his heel, that the two men embodied two radically different approaches to human survival could not be more salient. Chief Seke Mutema III, even in his fifties, possessed rippling muscles, a barrel chest and washboard stomach. He had trained in the U.S. Army and seen action in Iraq and Afghanistan. It was his knowledge and capabilities that had seen the chiefdom through Marauder attacks and famine.

In sharp contrast, Muchenjeri had a body that statistically

should have never survived at all. Yet, it housed a mind that had guided the chiefdom towards increasing mastery over its ravaged environment.

"My people!" Chief Seke Mutema III began, scanning the sea of faces. "I have seen fit that we cut through the formalities. Most of you know by now that Marauders have been seen in the west, headed this way. It is estimated that they will be here in two days. It seems that our great scientist and educator, Muchenjeri, has saved the day for us! Had he not instructed us to build these sand ships, we would not have the means to escape. But they are ready, just in time for when we need them."

The crowd rose in a murmur.

"Your lord is still speaking!" Simbarashe, Chiga and the chief's nephew, the effective protocol officer said.

"Muchenjeri, wise man, my brother-in-law, you are the Joseph to my Pharaoh!" Chief Seke Mutema turned to face Muchenjeri as a round of applause and ululation rose from the crowd.

"My lord is generous with his praise," said Muchenjeri, when the applause had died down. "What we have achieved here is the fruits of your astute leadership." He paused, noting how the granite features of his brother-in-law's face relaxed almost imperceptibly, and a glow came to his eyes. "However, having been given the floor, I must ask my lord to reconsider the decision to flee."

A gasp rose from the crowd. They knew when to participate in democracy, and when to be spectators. The objective of today's session was not to establish a consensus. It was for the two factions to finally have it out.

"If we flee, where do we go?" said Muchenjeri, addressing the crowd.

"North, where many people and wildlife have migrated to!" someone said. "Where there may still be abundant free-flowing water."

"If there are more people, might they not pose a bigger threat than the Marauders that we might be running away from?" Muchenjeri asked.

"Our sand ships will give us a tactical advantage," said Chief Seke Mutema III.

"I designed them to be vessels for trade!" said Muchenjeri. "For the planting of seeds and saplings over a wider area."

"Obviously, they can be useful in other ways," said Rinocheka, the head of security. He too had fought in international wars. "Let's not waste time; who wants to follow the chief in search of new lands to conquer and alliances we can negotiate from a position of power, or wait here passively for the law of the jungle to take them?"

Muchenjeri counted fourteen people with their hands down. He met the bewildered look on Munaku's face with an empathic nod.

"My brother-in-law," said Chief Seke Mutema III, "It looks like you will remain behind with your little intelligentsia clique. No hard feelings, everyone has the right to choose their own path for survival." He rose. "We will leave at first light tomorrow, but I will send a scout team ahead this afternoon."

"Wait!" cried Mugove, the treasurer. "What property shall we leave them, my chief?"

Five hundred pairs of eyes riveted towards Muchenjeri. It gratified him to note that he was at least allowed to negotiate on this.

"Their precious books and computers," said Chief Seke Mutema III. "Food to last them till the next harvest. Good luck keeping that away from the Marauders."

"And our seeds, please?" Chiga spoke for the first time. "And one sand ship …"

"No sand ship!" said the chief. "We cannot leave a working one here. If the Marauders find it, it will not be long before they can imitate the technology. We mean to get a head start in our migration."

"We agree!" said Muchenjeri.

• • •

The Technocrats stood on the highest *dwala*, under a tent, and watched the migration of Chief Seke Mutema III. There was something purposeful and adventurous in the way the sails unfurled in the fiery morning wind. Then, to whoops of delight, the giant misshapen metal beetles seemed to come to life, like specimens reorienting themselves after their collector had grown bored with and released them back into the garden.

Slowly, the sand ships cleared the school sports field, gaining momentum when they reached a dip in the ground. It was nearly an hour before they were just a speck on the shimmering horizon.

"We must begin our own preparations!" said Muchenjeri.

The Technocrats gathered around him eagerly. They had not dared initiate a discussion about the future while the larger faction was still here. They had trusted their natural leader.

"If we set out this afternoon, we can be in Chitungwiza. We can find materials with which to build new sand ships. I mean for us to go round from Chitungwiza. That way, we will avoid the Marauders as they pursue the chief and his group."

"You are confident that they will follow?" asked Hove.

"Of course, they will," said Handina, his wife. "Once they come here, they will see that this is a recently vacated but large settlement. The potential booty is impossible to dismiss as unobtainable. Which is why I am pleased that Muchenjeri doesn't want us to be around when the Marauders come."

"Well, let's get moving, then!" said Muchenjeri.

Munaku and five other young men stepped forward to move his stepfather onto a litter, which would be let down the *dwala* by ropes.

"Baba, you are so sure we can still survive here?" said Munaku, glancing around at the bleak landscape. "How? Why? The chief and his followers took everything."

"They took everything we made, son," said Muchenjeri. "But they did not take away the intellect, the work ethics, the human capital that made that everything. They left us with that, and we can utilize it to carry on taming our environment. That sand ship technology can be applied to other things, like irrigation, as you have all seen in our latest projects."

"But if we build again, what will stop Chief Seke Mutema III or any of the Marauders from coming back to seize by force anything they can get their hands on?" another youth—Muchenjeri could not recall her name—asked.

He smiled. "My daughter, are you confident that my brother-in-law will have those ships for long? Factor in the many variables; no one among them knows how to build a sand ship from scratch, let alone repair one. They moved away from a source of raw materials. Battles with other groups might decimate the few technically minded members of their group, whereas we will continue to avoid war because we haven't got the means to fight one."

"I see what you mean, *Baba*!" said Munaku, with alacrity. "Our little group represents not only the accumulation of human knowledge but also its survival to the next generation."

Muchenjeri beamed at him. He would make a great leader one day. In addition to his education and training, Munaku had his uncle's physique. He would make a formidable warrior should the need arise.

The sun glared fiercely on them as it had done for so many years. But they would survive it. Muchenjeri did not feel the ground when his feet touched it. He sank into his wheelchair, and stared out to the horizon.

# ABOUT THE AUTHOR

Masimba Musodza was born in Zimbabwe, but has lived most of his adult life in the UK, settling in the North East England town of Middlesbrough. His short fiction, mostly on the speculative fiction spectrum, has appeared in anthologies and periodicals around the world and online. He has published two novels and a novella in ChiShona, his first language, and a collection of short stories in English. Internet Speculative Fiction Database author record #230825

# THE LONGEST BREATH

## Lisa Beebe

AYUKO hadn't spoken aloud since Mina brought her to Seven Palms nearly a month earlier. She was angry at her daughter for forcing her to leave Japan for Florida. At the same time, she resented Mina, her only child, for not making more frequent visits to the retirement home.

Ayuko avoided interacting with the Seven Palms staff and the other residents by pretending she didn't understand English. She was frustrated with all of them for not speaking any Japanese. At first, the staff made an effort to communicate with her, introducing her to the other seniors. She remembered a few of their names, even if she'd never said them out loud. Sarah. Ana. Destiny. George. Kay.

Ayuko spent most of her days sitting alone in her room. Her window looked toward the new shoreline, where the main road headed straight into the bay. Downhill from Seven Palms, there had been a river and the rest of the town. Now, there was just brackish water.

Six months earlier, before Ayuko arrived, what the meteorologists referred to as a "thousand-year flood" had swallowed the town. When the waters from the bay flowed upstream, flooding the banks of the river, everyone evacuated in a hurry. The water kept coming, covering whole houses. Days passed, and then weeks, without the water level returning to normal. Aside from minor tidal changes, it wasn't going anywhere.

From her window, Ayuko could see the steeple of a church. She had never seen the church itself, but she could tell if the tide was high or low by how much of the steeple was visible.

The view made her sad, and she was glad Shin hadn't lived to see it. Her husband had worked as a fisherman for many years, and after he retired and sold his boat, he had never been the same. A year later, he looked like he'd aged ten years. The doctors said his death was due to a heart attack, but Ayuko believed he had simply given up.

Sometimes she was tempted to give up, too, but her heart kept beating anyway. Ayuko was eighty-two, and back in Japan, she'd felt like she still had plenty of living to do. There, she was a free diver, swimming deep down on a single breath of air and bringing up pearl after pearl. She had been diving since she was a girl, following in her ancestors' footsteps, until her own daughter put a stop to it.

"You can't keep putting your body through that," Mina had said. "It's too dangerous for someone your age." She insisted on bringing Ayuko to the United States, claiming she wanted her close by. Then, instead of letting Ayuko live with her and her husband, as tradition dictated, Mina had moved her mother into Seven Palms.

At night, in her dreams, Ayuko left her lonely, sterile room behind. She inhaled deeply and descended into the blue depths where she had spent so many years. When she awoke, she exhaled with a frustrated huff, returning unwillingly to the surface and to the dry dullness of her waking life.

Each day, one of the nurses escorted Ayuko to the TV lounge, while speaking to her slowly in English about how important it was to be social. Other residents walked to the shopping plaza up the street in the afternoons, but Ayuko sat in the lounge with the residents who were too incapacitated to leave. She found shopping in the giant American stores exhausting. Instead, she sat in silence, watching whatever the other residents put on the TV until the nurses let her return to her room.

Ayuko wasn't the only new resident who disliked the home. Thousands of people had been displaced by the flood. Several of the older townspeople had rented rooms at Seven Palms, planning to stay only until their houses were once again habitable. It now seemed unlikely that day would ever come.

Mina had negotiated a good deal on Ayuko's rent, since her room overlooked the flood. This was a view many of the new residents found depressing. Outside of the home, the road leading into the water was blocked off with orange pylons and a big sign that read: "No Admittance." Local residents weren't allowed to swim—or even take boats—through the area, since the flood had left it full of toxic chemicals and hidden obstacles.

One afternoon, it was raining, and many of the residents skipped their daily shopping trip to stay in the lounge and play cards or Scrabble. A few of the locals whose homes had been claimed by the floodwaters talked about what they missed most.

"My photo of Norm," said a woman with curly white hair, "I kept it by my bed and always kissed it goodnight. I will never forgive myself for not packing it."

"Did you live close by?" a lady named Kay asked.

"So close. Palm and 3rd. The yellow house kitty-corner from the New Hope Church. It'd be a two-minute walk from here if there wasn't any water."

A nurse named Steven had been listening in. He asked, "Have you looked into hiring one of those resurfacing teams? I hear they do a great job of bringing stuff up and cleaning it."

The woman nodded, "They charge thousands of dollars. It's such a racket. Only licensed resurfacers are allowed in the water, so it's the only way to get your stuff back. I don't have that kind of money, and the insurance company won't cover it. It's an act of god, they say."

"I tell you, I wouldn't want to get in that water, even with all the safety gear they wear," said Steven. "My girlfriend works at the hospital, and they've had people coming in with that brain-eating amoeba thing. It used to only get people in fresh water, but all of the patients admitted they'd gone in the floodwaters. The doctors think the amoeba mutated. It can survive in saltier water now, and it kills almost everyone it infects. Get a little of that water up your nose, and you're a goner."

Ayuko resisted the temptation to roll her eyes. Only an amateur got water in her nose while diving.

The woman sighed, "What *isn't* in that nasty water?"

"Manatees," said Kay softly, and everybody got quiet, remembering that the slow-moving mammals were now believed extinct. The latest floods had been the last straw, destroying all of their remaining habitat.

The curly-haired woman sighed again, "We lost so much. I know it's just stuff, but I miss that picture. It hurts to think about it starting to dissolve."

"It may seem vain but I miss my pearls," said Kay. "They belonged to my grandmother and I wore them on my wedding day. Now my granddaughter is engaged and I just wish ..." Her voice trailed off.

It was the mention of pearls that put the idea in Ayuko's head. She'd spent her life diving for them, and she couldn't help wondering, could she do it one more time? She wasn't afraid of the pollution or the unfamiliar location. What did she have to lose? She missed the dives and how alive they made her feel. She missed the sense of focus that came from controlling her breath. She missed the way the water pressed against her body when she was down deep.

*I could dive out there,* she thought to herself. But could she really?

During the day, the staff monitored the residents' whereabouts, expecting them to check in and out at the front desk. At night, she might be able to sneak out, but she'd never be able to find her way around underwater. She would need a light.

The next afternoon, Ayuko signed herself out for the first time and walked to the Target in the shopping plaza. In the sporting goods section, she found an empty aisle and a taped-up sign: "By order of the health department, we are unable to sell diving masks and equipment until further notice. All local diving areas are closed to the public due to pollution."

Ayuko had never worn a mask to dive. She didn't like the way they fogged up, making it hard to see, or the marks they left around her eyes when she took them off. In the next aisle, amid the biking and hiking supplies, she found what she was looking for: a waterproof headlamp.

She paid for it in cash, just in case Mina was tracking her spending.

Ayuko went to bed early and set an alarm on her phone for 1 a.m. When it woke her, she dug through her dresser for her swimsuit, but it wasn't in any of the drawers. Mina must have taken it, probably to prevent a situation like this. Ayuko shook her head. That settled it.

She would dive without a suit.

She put on her robe and slippers, tucked the headlamp into her pocket, and walked quietly down the hallway. If anyone saw her, she would act confused, head for the kitchen, and make a cup of decaffeinated tea. Nobody spotted her. Ayuko slipped out the side door and propped it open with a small rock to prevent it from locking behind her.

A minute later, she stood at the water's edge. She put on the headlamp, tightening the strap until it was snug, but left the light turned off. She removed her robe, folded it neatly, and tucked it under a bush with her slippers.

Looking out at the water, she took a deep breath. It smelled wrong. A little salty, but there was something else there. Something rotten. Something toxic.

She stepped forward into it and was surprised at its warmth. She walked in deeper, stepping gingerly, because she couldn't see the bottom. When the water was up to her waist, she swam toward the church steeple. She was grateful that the curly-haired woman's home was near one of the submerged neighbourhood's only visible landmarks. When she neared it, she turned on the lamp and ducked her head beneath the surface. The water was too murky to see much, so she dived down farther to get a sense of how the block was oriented.

When she saw the yellow house, it occurred to her that she didn't have a plan for getting inside. The doors and windows were probably locked and held even more tightly shut by the soaked, swollen wood. She hoped she wouldn't have to break in.

She surfaced for a quick breath, then swam down again to take a closer look. That's when she noticed an upstairs window had been left open. The woman must have left in a hurry during the first evacuation and forgotten to close it.

Ayuko popped the window screen out and laid it carefully on the roof. Then she returned to the surface.

She would need more air this time. She turned the headlamp off and floated there for a few minutes, looking up at the stars. She breathed deeply, letting her body relax as she mentally prepared for the dive. She was naked and the night air was cool, but the goosebumps on her arms were from excitement.

When she felt ready, she inhaled until her chest was full, flicked on the headlamp, and began her dive. When she reached the house, she swam through the open window and down a wide hallway. She found the master bedroom at the end of the hall.

Ayuko had never been in an underwater house before, and the experience was disconcerting. In the dark expanse of water, the bedroom felt small, but compared to her bedroom in Japan, it was massive. The size felt wasteful to Ayuko, another example of American excess.

When she saw the small blue and white ceramic frame on the bedside table, she remembered the purpose of her dive. The photo looked intact, so she picked it up and returned down the hallway. She swam out the window, approaching the surface.

When she emerged, she was proud of herself for barely needing to catch her breath. The dive had been easier than she'd expected. She swam to shore with the frame in one hand.

When she reached the shore, she used the robe as a towel,

and then put it on. She returned the headlamp to one pocket and slipped the frame into the other. She pulled her wet hair into a tight bun.

She had gotten away with it.

Standing there, looking out at the dark water, it occurred to her that she hadn't encountered even a single fish. Was anything left alive out there? She might never know for sure—unless she returned for another swim.

Despite her concern for the sea life, Ayuko's spirit was buoyed by the thought of future swims and by the knowledge that at some point the following day, she would sneak the little frame onto the curly-haired woman's bedside table.

She headed back up to Seven Palms. Once again, she had a plan. If a night nurse stopped her, she would act as if she didn't understand the rules. She made it back to her room unnoticed, the night nurses busy elsewhere.

Ayuko turned on the light and inspected the small ceramic frame. She rinsed it in her bathroom sink and carefully removed the photo from the frame so they could dry separately. Then she took a shower and went to bed. She dreamt of being back underwater.

By morning, the photo was dry. She was surprised at how well it had survived the six-month submersion. She put it back in the frame and tucked it into her bag. Then she got dressed and headed to the cafeteria. She knew she was carrying something precious.

As usual, the woman behind the breakfast counter said, "Good morning."

For once, Ayuko didn't ignore her. She said, "Good morning," and smiled.

# ABOUT THE AUTHOR

Lisa Beebe lives in Los Angeles, where she sometimes talks to the ocean. Her work has appeared in *Five South*, *HAD*, *Indiana Review*, *Psychopomp*, and *Vestal Review*, among others. Her story, "I (Palm Tree) Los Angeles," was selected for the 2022 Wigleaf Top 50.

# NO ROOM AT WORLD'S END

## Shiksha Dheda

MY shoulders widen: they broaden, outstretch the backs of your valleys. My fingers lengthen, my legs grow heftier. They expand, they grow; taking up too much space in this room. You wince at my cigarette smoke. It's a grey mistress dancing seductively, swaying in the unclean air to her own mindless rhythm. She smears grey ash on all her enthralled onlookers; they wait (with polluted breath) for just one chance to dance with her, to sway to her destructive spins.

I can outrun you now. My legs have been made stronger by technological advances and traversing the near insurmountable task of space. I run wild on the playground of galaxies, conquering planet after planet, pinning my maps, and spreading the seeds of my progress.

I am strong now. I've grown from a measly tiny fish, then

walked on all fours. I finally climbed trees and then, then I discovered science. I've learned so much, yet there is so much more to learn, to do.

I thought I would be able to carry you now. I thought I could put my hardened palms in the cups of your porcelain pits. I figured I could lift you up like a rag doll. You, being weakened and eroded by the rivers of age and hard work.

But, my shoulders are too broad now and my fingers are too lengthy. My legs are too hefty and the grey mistress weighs down on my lungs now—skirting through my veins, darkening my green with her grey streaks.

I can't stop growing now: my shoulders, my legs, my fingers all too large now. Space has no room for me, you have run out of patience for me and I am running,

running out of time.

# ABOUT THE AUTHOR

Shiksha Dheda is a South African of Indian descent. She uses writing to express her OCD and depression roller-coaster ventures, but mostly to avoid working on her master's degree. Sometimes, she dabbles in photography, painting, and baking lopsided layered cakes.

Her writing has been featured (on/forthcoming) in *Wigleaf, Passages North, Brittle Paper, Door is a jar* and *Epoch Press* amongst others. She is the Pushcart nominated author of *Washed Away* (Alien Buddha Press, 2021).

She rambles annoyingly at Twitter: @ShikshaWrites. You can find (or ignore her) at shikshadheda.wixsite.com/writing

# SHAPING LAKES AND HONEYCAKES

## Wendy Nikel

MELIA stood upon the shores of the receding lake, shaping her tale for the meagre audience of children and elders. Storyshaping always came easier when there were more listeners, but this was her third attempt this moon cycle at reshaping the lake's story, with little to show for her efforts; she couldn't blame the others for not taking time out of their workdays to listen in anymore.

"... and the haze melted away like a fog," Melia said in a hush, spreading her arms wide. "The waters swelled, crisp and clear. The fish returned, and the children rushed to the shallows to cool themselves in its freshness."

Some of the elders closed their eyes and smiled in remembrance, but the children nearest the water just stared at the grimy pool with wrinkled noses, watching half-heartedly for the storyshaping to take effect.

The waters rippled, catching a glimmer of sunlight, and Melia's heart leapt in unguarded hope—Would it work this time? Would the lake be restored?—but the movement was only due to a fishing boat approaching from around the cape, leaving an oily slick of residue in its wake.

Melia's shoulders fell.

Sensing that the story was over, some of the children leapt to their feet, chasing one another around and skipping rocks and discarded bottle caps across the lake's surface.

Melia gathered the pages of her story, crumpling them in her fists.

Aunt Nelly reached out to stop her. "It's a good story, love."

"But it didn't work. It was supposed to change things." Melia had worked so hard on selecting just the right words and descriptions. Lately she'd been practicing more, perfecting her tone and cadences by shaping stories about sky-blue frogs and lizards that hummed and sunflowers that produced giant heads of rock candy until her garden was teeming with the fantastical creatures and sugary sweets. These trivial things she could storyshift so easily—and she made a decent living doing so—but the lake was somehow just too much. Too big, too important, or perhaps too badly ruined.

Offshore, the fishermen pulled in their net. It slipped aboard too easily, without a single fish to weigh it down. How much longer would their village sustain them without any fish? And what then? Where would they go? What would they do?

"Have you asked your mother about it?" Aunt Nelly asked, smoothing out a wrinkled page. "She did always have a way with words."

Melia scowled. Her mother had once been known as one of the region's most skilled storyshapers, but she'd abandoned it all—stories, the village, and her only daughter—years ago in favour of a solitary cabin high in the mountains. Melia had been preoccupied with her own training at the time, but the longer the two went without discussing the reasons for her departure, the harder it was to broach the topic.

Still, when Melia had written to her weeks ago and mentioned in passing the trouble with the lake, Mother's response had—as always—passed over any topic having to do with storyshaping.

Maybe Aunt Nelly was onto something, though. Maybe it was time to visit Mother, face-to-face.

• • •

It was quicker to travel by story, so the next morning, Melia pressed her nicest travelling dress, sat in her garden, and shaped a thrilling tale of traversing forests and rivers and climbing the soaring mountains to bring Mother a basket of her favourite honeycakes. When Melia opened her eyes, she stood upon the cabin's threshold, the basket of sweets in her hand.

Her mother frowned, her arms crossed, before her. "You

might as well come in."

Mother's cabin was small but cozy and filled with all sorts of peculiar odds and ends: abandoned bird nests, river-smoothed stones, stout walking sticks. But no books.

Melia held out the honeycakes as a peace offering.

"You made these yourself?" Mother asked.

"I shaped them."

Mother frowned. "Even you should know that storyshaped food lacks sustenance."

Melia lowered her eyes. If she'd stopped to think of Mother's predilections, she'd have realized it'd have been better to bake them by hand. Already, she was regretting this visit.

"They lack sustenance," Mother continued, "just as your feet lack blisters and your muscles lack the satisfying ache of knowing that they have conquered this mountain."

"Is that why you don't tell stories anymore?" Melia blurted out. "You prefer the toil?"

"No, I realized that there are times when it is better to speak hard truths than to fill the world with more comforting lies."

"You grew cynical."

"I grew wise."

"I came to ask you for your help," Melia said, her temper rising, "not to have my work disparaged. The lake—it's dying. Don't you even care?"

"Perhaps it's not the lake that needs reshaping," Mother said, "but you."

Melia rose, ready to storm off, but Mother opened a jar and held out a honeycake of her own. It smelled fresh. Homemade. More appealing than Melia's storyshaped ones.

"Go ahead," Mother said. "Take one for your journey home."

It'd been ages since Melia had tasted one of Mother's honeycakes, and the mere aroma stirred up memories of sticky summer afternoons in a simpler time, when all Melia had had to worry about was getting home by dinnertime and planning the next day's adventures. Reluctantly, Melia reached into the jar. She took a bite, and it flaked apart on her tongue. The buttery treat melted away in her mouth, leaving behind soft vestiges of sweetness, which she sought out with her tongue between all the crevices of her teeth.

"I'm sorry I couldn't help you," Mother said, placing the lid on the jar.

Melia's mouth watered, aching for another honeycake, but she had other things on her mind now. She glanced out the window to where the rocky path wound down the mountain. It did look like a treacherous path—the exact sort that her younger self would have been eager to conquer.

"Thank you," she muttered. "You might have helped me after all."

If she left now, she could be home by dark.

• • •

It took great effort to convince the villagers to meet her at the lake, but eventually, they set aside their work and came.

Melia stood before them with trembling knees. If only

they'd hear her out …

"Today's story isn't about the lake," she said, willing her voice to carry across the crowd.

"Then why are we here?" someone shouted.

"I thought you were going to fix this!"

"The story I'm telling today is about us." Melia took a deep breath. "You see, people can't be shaped as easily as rocks and trees and frogs and honeycakes. People need to accept the shaping and allow it to happen. So please, just listen, and ask yourself: who do I want to be?"

And she wove a tale, heartfelt and aching, unlike any they'd heard before. Not about the lake or the village around them as they wanted them to be, but about people she saw each day and what they might become. People who were unafraid to gather only what they needed and leave the rest for others, for another day. People who were unhurried and patient and kind, even when it meant more work. People who savoured the joys of discovery and satisfaction of a job well done. People who valued humanity over property, and the gathering of wisdom over the gathering of wealth.

The village listened to her story of people. People that they could become.

When she was finished, Melia turned around, unable to keep the tears from her eyes and terrified that, in their stubbornness, the village might resent her storyshaping. Would it work this time? Would they listen?

Out on the lake, the waters rippled, catching a glimmer of sunlight, and this time, that sparkle of hope didn't fade.

# ABOUT THE AUTHOR

Wendy Nikel is a speculative fiction author with a degree in elementary education, a fondness for road trips, and a terrible habit of forgetting where she's left her cup of tea. Her short fiction has been published by *Analog, Beneath Ceaseless Skies, Nature*, and elsewhere. Her time travel novella series, beginning with *The Continuum*, is available from World Weaver Press. For more info, visit wendynikel.com.

# DRAWING THE LINE

## Gustavo Bondoni

Yevgeny cursed under his breath.

Philippa smiled. "Things not going to plan?" the elderly woman asked.

"Things never go to plan." He held up a mangled piece of aluminum alloy. "I'll need to take this back to the shop and try to use it as a pattern to machine a new one." He held it higher, trying to see how the light went through compound curves of the tube. "I don't think it's going to be easy."

"I trust you," Philippa said.

He knew she did. That was why he'd find a way, some way, any way of getting it done.

They sat in silence for a few minutes. The morning sun wasn't as harsh as it would be at noontime, and he could bask in it, even with his pale skin.

Then, disaster. Siti walked past, smiled and nodded, her red shuka tightly wrapped around her, her head erect, the inevitable walking stick, as thin and straight as she was, held in one hand.

He sighed as Siti disappeared around a corner.

"You should tell her how you feel," Philippa said. "You might be surprised."

Yevgeny groaned. *Was it that obvious to everyone?* "Of course. The woman changing the face of Africa, creating technologies that are pushing back the effects of global warming, must just be dying to hear all about how the mechanic has a crush on her."

"So you're afraid, then."

"Shouldn't I be? She's a great visionary. I'm fixing your blender so you can drink margaritas."

"And yet, you don't seem afraid of me. Or of Oscar. He told me you fixed his shower last week."

"I ..."

"Have you forgotten who we are?"

"No. Of course not. No one on Earth will ever forget you." He realized that sounded as if they were about to die. "I mean ..."

"I know what you mean. I was young once, too." She put a finger on his mouth to keep him from speaking. "You say that she is changing the world. That's true. But I already have, and you don't have any problems talking to me. Oscar ... Oscar has probably saved more lives than anyone alive. His seed stock broke the corporate monopoly ... and he was the person who finally negotiated the completion of the Great Green Wall. He is as important as Siti could ever hope to be."

"I guess you're right."

"Do you know what Oscar says about you? He says he wished you were his son."

It was true. The octogenarian scientist had said it to Yevgeny himself more than once.

"That's just because I do him favours sometimes."

"No. If you only did him favours, he wouldn't have said anything. It's because you do everyone favours. My blender. The gardener's pinball machine. None of these things are what you're being paid for. We all know that. And yet you take the time necessary to do them for us."

"Yeah. I guess. Maybe my problem is that the director doesn't need any favours."

• • •

The sun was now straight overhead. Yevgeny—though it made him feel that he was too delicate for Africa—wore a cowboy hat. It felt ridiculous to be wearing it within a stone's throw of the Sahara desert in Chad, but somehow a British pith helmet would have seemed monstrously colonial. Nothing else he'd tried worked for him; killing heat was never something he'd worried about in Petrozavodsk. Back home, you wore hats to keep your ears from freezing.

Despite the broiling air, he pedalled hard. The motor he'd had to repair—an irrigation pump—had taken much longer than anticipated, and lunch would be served in fifteen minutes. He'd already lost any chance of washing up, and lunch was the one meal that no one would ever dare to miss, or one would face the director's wrath.

Fortunately, the road had just been paved with a kind of

biodegradable rubber that, compared to the old dirt track, made him feel like he was moving at a million miles an hour.

He skidded to a halt in front of the gleaming reflective glass of the administration building, dropped the bike on the ground and checked his watch. He was late, but not terminally so.

He turned to run towards the Shady Vale, the grassy depression surrounded by trees that served as a communal cafeteria, when he noticed Jennifer Ward exiting the building carrying a pair of folders under her arm. When she saw him she looked as flustered as he felt. But that was understandable: his own tardiness would be forgiven due to distance and complexity; hers would cause comment.

He gave her an encouraging smile. "Come on. Maybe if we both walk in together, she'll go easy on us."

Jennifer laughed, a nervous sound, and put the folders in her backpack. "I hope you're right."

As they filed between the tables, every eye followed them. There was no way around it, but maybe he could draw the fire himself and allow Jennifer to find her place unnoticed. He stopped in front of the director's table and addressed Siti. "I'm sorry I'm late. The pump took longer than I expected."

To his relief, she nodded her approval. "But it's working now?"

"Yes. And it should stay that way."

"Good. That pump is critical for the Line."

The Line. Everyone else in the world called it the Great Green Wall of Africa, a barrier of trees several kilometres wide just south of the Sahara. It had been credited for holding back the expansion of the desert through the worst spasms of the Climate Crises. The people who'd worked there in the past fifty years, heroes like Philippa and Oscar, had called it the Front Line ... and the name, at least the "Line" part of it, had stuck. Now, the complex, once a central administrative node for the tree-planting project, was working on a completely different kind of climate change technology, but they were still on the bleeding edge.

"I know."

"Thanks for taking care of it."

"It was my pleasure." He turned to find his seat. It would have been randomly assigned, so he might have to search for it.

"Yevgeny?"

"Yes?" he turned back.

"Why don't you take a buggy for yourself? They're all solar, so they don't pollute, you know."

She was teasing him, of course. He was the one who kept the complex's cars running. "I'm fine with the bicycle. It keeps me in shape, and it's not as if it ever rains around here."

Now he was teasing her, and the faces around the table registered surprise. First he was late, and now this.

But Siti took the barb in stride. "For now," she replied.

• • •

"Yes," Yevgeny told Adjo impatiently. "I know it's supposed to be in stock. I can read an inventory just as well as you can.

But it's not there."

"What did you use it for?"

"I didn't use it. Someone else must have taken it."

"That's silly. You're the only one who needs those."

The piece of flat glass he needed was not something he'd have forgotten he used. It was the smallest high-efficiency photovoltaic variably transparent piece of glass in the world, created in the lab across the path by the only people who knew how to build it. But more importantly, it was a circle thirty centimetres across that only fit onto the skylight at the top of the office area, to shine light straight onto the director's desk. The climb up to that particular point of the roof was a nightmare, and he'd put off attempting it until Siti really got on his case.

And when she did, the niche holding the replacement part was empty.

"I think someone stole it," Yevgeny said.

That shocked the other man. "Who would do such a thing?"

"How should I know? Maybe someone who wants to reverse-engineer one of the most advanced pieces of technology on the planet?"

"Look. If you lost it, just say so. I'm sure the lab will build you another one. They like to show off."

"I'm telling you, I didn't lose it, I didn't break it, and I most certainly am not going to let this one pass. If we have a thief in the colony, or someone working for one of the corporations, we need to find out who it is."

Adjo still seemed unconcerned. "It's just a piece of glass."

Yevgeny sighed. "I know it doesn't sound like much, but it's the key to a lot of things. If one of the corporations gets ahead of our research cycle, it could undo years of good. Now kick this one up the ladder, will you?"

Adjo nodded. "All right. I still think it's a waste of time, but if you feel it's important, I'll take it up with the director. But don't blame me if she ignores it."

"Thank you." His supervisor could often be slow about technological issues, but once he gave his word, it was as good as gold. He would take it up, and make the case for an investigation as best he could.

Yevgeny walked back to his workshop, cursing the paper-white skin that kept him under cover unless he was slathered in sunscreen. He'd made the mistake, just a couple weeks before, of believing that he'd been in Africa long enough that he could work without a shirt. The resulting blistering and lobster-coloured skin had been painful, but not as much as the condescending kindness of the men and women around him. Even the other non-Africans seemed to do better in the sun than Yevgeny, but the response that hurt the most was Siti's understanding smile and assurances that he'd get used to the sun eventually, but that he should probably work up to that point, using ever-lower SPF factors until he found the one that worked for him.

At least the workshop was a beautiful place to spend one's working day. Open to the breeze on three sides— although the glass doors could be closed when needed—the structure appeared to have been built out of gossamer and spiderwebs. Thin metal tracings, interwoven with the surrounding trees, supported a solar roof array that powered all his equipment. For delicate jobs that required a dust-proof environment, a paint and work cabin was tucked behind the workbenches, which, themselves, had been built of wood from the Green Wall.

Troubled by the loss of the panel, Yevgeny went back into the storage area—basically just a big closet behind the paint cabin—with a datapad on whose screen the inventory list was displayed. He spent his afternoon checking every single cubbyhole. His stock of screws and minor parts was way off, but that was his own fault. He never remembered to update the inventory when he used those—he was always in a hurry, and who would worry about a couple of bolts here or a T-bracket there?

The rest of the inventory looked OK, even the expensive drone parts, except ... there was a solar supercooler missing that he didn't recall having fitted onto anything. This was a part about the size of a datapad whose function was to turn the energy of the ever-present sunlight into electricity that ran a powerful compact cooling system. It was eminently portable, but also obsolete—Siti's drones had begun to carry a new version, lighter and more powerful, when they went up and, since none of those had broken yet, he hadn't asked the lab for replacement parts.

Then he smacked his head. "Yevgeny," he reminded himself. "You are an idiot. That is why you will always only be a mechanic."

The supercooler was only obsolete there, in that small village of less than five hundred people who worked and lived in the complex. The lab—run by twenty material scientists, complete with teams of assistants, who'd come from all over the world to work under Oscar and Philippa, and who now reported to Siti—held some of the most advanced manufacturing equipment anywhere. But more importantly than that, the researchers within knew what to do with their machines. Anywhere else on the planet, the missing part would be the most advanced compact cooling device anyone had ever seen.

Even Yevgeny was hesitant to take apart components delivered from the lab. Of course, after he grew familiar with how they functioned, he would usually attempt a dissection ... but semiconductors and superconducters were not something he could fix with a wrench, even if he understood how they worked in conjunction with the rest of the electronics around them.

Well, at least he would become obsolete with his eyes open.

In the meantime, he needed to think. The supercooler was likely long gone, mailed out of the complex through their community courier service, but he wanted to try to figure out who'd had the opportunity to take the missing parts before he went to Adjo again. He thought best while either working or on his bike ... and it wasn't time for his ride just yet.

There were only a couple of jobs left to do. The first was

to replace the nav chip on one of the buggies. That, due to some boneheaded design or a misguided belief that nav chips would never fail, was an arduous task that involved removing a good chunk of the forward bulkhead.

Yevgeny whistled a tune and began dismantling the car. He tried to understand who might have a reason to take things from the complex. Most thefts, he knew from having spent his early childhood during Russia's Transition, came from a lack of money. That, of course, might still be a good motive, but in the complex—and in Chad itself, and in the rest of the Wall Treaty Nations—money was no longer used. He believed that the nearest place that still used any kind of currency was Senegal, but he couldn't be sure. Then what? Nationalism? That was still alive and well, even after the Consolidation ... but everyone was vetted thoroughly before they were allowed to remain.

He had a hard time coming to any conclusion and before he knew it, an hour had passed and he was done with the chip. He looked up at the wall display ...

Time for his ride.

The complex was a melting pot of several religions. The Christians went to church—a long and dusty ride—every Sunday, and the Muslim majority had several prayer halts each day. Yevgeny had only one sacred ritual: every evening, at exactly six in the evening, he'd drop everything and take a one-hour bike ride along the paths and roads around the complex and the airfield. It was the one period of the day when his comm was off, and he wouldn't do anyone any favours. The cool predusk wind, humid and, if not quite brisk at least less hot, represented glorious relief from the oppressive heat.

And he left at six o'clock precisely even if that meant, as it did on that day, that Philippa would only get her blender working again tomorrow.

His mind worried the problem of the missing parts, but he couldn't come to any conclusion. He knew everyone involved in the project and he couldn't imagine anyone betraying it. There were all sorts of people at the complex: friendly, taciturn, engaging, shy, sullen, even a few who were openly aggressive and disliked the decision to allow a Russian into the project—and took that out on Yevgeny himself. But even though he didn't get along with all of them, he couldn't imagine one being a traitor.

He arrived tired, sweaty and no closer to finding an answer than when he'd set out, to find Siti leaning against one of his workbenches. She'd abandoned her usual Maasai attire for a dark business suit which, if possible, made her look even more fabulous.

"I'm sorry you had to wait," he said. "I always take a ride at this time."

She smiled, perfect white teeth contrasting brilliantly with her skin. "I know. And it's always exactly one hour. I only just arrived a minute ago."

"Oh," he didn't know whether he should be worried or honoured that the director knew his habits. "Can I help you?"

"I have a couple of questions about the missing glass. I'll

make it quick, because I know you like to clean the workshop and shower before dinner."

"Don't rush on my account. It's pretty clean." He told her about the missing glass, and also about the cooling element.

She listened grimly. "Too much coincidence."

"That's what I thought, too."

"All right. We'll have to look into it, but that's not the reason I came here. Can you set up a charging station for the drones? I want to be able to charge all sixteen of them simultaneously and solar-only charge is taking too long."

He thought about it for a moment. The drones could charge in an hour using the sunlight that hit them, but could be back up in minutes using the current generated by the much larger solar arrays of the complex. "I think so. Do you want to test them all at once?"

"We're past that. I want to send them up with the grid."

The supercooled netting that made up the grid was meant to catch and condense moisture in the air.

"You're going to try to make it rain?"

There had been other efforts. Cloud seeding, static condensers. None of them had been successful on a large scale. The seeding, in fact, had failed completely, despite working perfectly in laboratory conditions. The lack of artificial rain, and their continued reliance on irrigation from groundwater was a running joke in the complex.

"Not yet. We need to test the full flight for a few weeks to see if they can hold the grid steady before we try to cool the grid." Her half smile told him that there was something she wasn't saying, but before he could ask, she went on. "How long do you think the charging station would take?"

"I suppose you want it somewhere without trees."

The smile widened. "That would probably be for the best, yes."

"I'll get to work on it tomorrow. I'll need to get some parts in from N'Djamena. I think probably ..." He did some calculations in his head. "Three days."

• • •

Yevgeny forgot all about the missing parts as the sudden rush of work enveloped him. First, he set out the wiring he would need for the charging station—he'd selected a flat, dusty stretch about four hundred metres from the complex—and, despite the irony of it, he made sure the cables were well waterproofed. He set up sixteen posts, well separated from one another. The only thing missing were the special cables that would plug into each of the drones—those were the parts he'd ordered.

The drive to the capital required—to his chagrin—that he borrow one of the buggies. He hated them because he didn't trust them ... it was spooky to think that the solar panels could power the vehicle with no fuel, no external power whatsoever. Even after the Transition, rural Russians trusted diesel with their lives ... solar was for city folk who weren't at risk of being stranded in the snow a hundred kilometres from anything.

So he put off borrowing the car. Instead, he spent a much

longer time than he should have machining the part for Philippa's blender. But there was only so much he could do to a curved tube half the size of his pinkie finger, and he was soon driving along the dusty road.

The surface was sealed with biodegradable oils, ideal for the lightweight, well-sprung buggies, but the trip still took a long time and brought back memories that Yevgeny preferred to suppress. He was a different person when he'd first arrived from Russia, via N'Djamena, along that same road. Then, his head had been full of misconceptions, even if his heart was in the right place.

The sight of an umbrella thorn acacia brought that day back to him in vivid detail. It hadn't even been that long ago. He'd hired a driver to bring him to the complex and, a few kilometres out, he'd seen an African woman walking steadily along the road.

He'd told the man to stop beside her and offered her a lift in tortured French. She'd declined with a smile, in English much better than his French—and also much better than his own English. Then he'd offered her food. She was tall and thin, and he thought she might be underfed. All he'd had was the remains of a hamburger from the McDonald's at the airport.

This had been rejected with a laugh and the explanation that people in Chad tended to eat a much healthier diet ... and preferred real meat in their burgers. She'd walked away, leaving him bemused.

He'd been even more bemused when the woman he'd

seen walking was introduced to him a few hours later as Dr. Siti Gisemba, the Kenyan Director of the complex ... and a legendary figure in her own right, despite being in her early thirties.

Talk about getting off on the wrong foot. The only good of it was that he knew he would never have a chance with her, so he didn't spend too much time dreaming.

Five hours later, Yevgeny returned to the complex. The parts had been waiting for him in the office building that the Green Wall project had in N'Djamena's modern downtown.

He would be able to finish constructing the charging station the following morning, and now he had a few minutes to spare before bicycle time came around. He headed straight for the small compound where retired members of the community lived in airy, beautiful houses surrounded by the living wall itself.

"I'm sorry this took so long," he told Philippa.

The woman just smiled. "I hear you've been busy."

He took the part he'd built and placed it in the open space left by the original. It was a nearly perfect match, but he wasn't satisfied. Philippa watched him fondly while he filed the part until it was a precise match.

"You know," she said, "I never thought you would fit in here. You looked too young, too eager to change things. I thought the rigid structure would get to you and you'd leave after a few months. But you're here to stay, aren't you?"

"What do you mean?"

"Not every young man from ... your background ... can

live with the rules."

"You mean sitting down to lunch at exactly the same time?"

"Of course. That and the fact that you exchange all your working hours for nothing other than room and board. Everyone here would be extremely well paid on the open market."

He shrugged. "I've been on the open market. There's nothing you can buy that compares to living here. I was scared it might not be all that was promised. My main worry was that Africa might be like the old movies. But this ... this is paradise."

"If Siti has her way, the whole world will be like this someday. Most of Africa already is, as well as South America and Australia."

He smiled. "Russia ... may take a while."

"Maybe less than you think. There are a lot of initiatives already in place. Most of the big cities are getting there. We're actually much more worried about Western Europe and North America."

"They seem to do all right."

"Perhaps, but by keeping up a monetary economy, they are actually slowing their pace of development and falling behind. Their people are doing well, but they're still missing out." She shook her head. "Part of that is the fact that they're afraid to change, of course. But another part is that the environmental groups have grown too radicalized. You don't get harmony like this by beating people over the head and blowing up banks. You don't get it by using unlicensed technology to replace what communities are already using—and causing accidents that kill the very people you're trying to convert. Harmony comes naturally from showing everyone how nice it is … and by being together. That's the real reason Siti forces us all to be punctual for lunch and dinner." Philippa's eyes twinkled. "She used to really, really hate being tied down for two hours. If it was up to her, she'd work all day without stopping."

"So she does it for us."

"Of course. And we do it for us, as well. And so do you. I've seen you pedalling furiously from miles away to arrive in time to wash before eating. You belong here because you understand … and even if you didn't understand the reasons behind the insistence until now, you never had to be reminded about the rule, and you never acted as if it was stupid."

He finished adjusting the part and pressed the outer casing back in place. Then he tested the blender and was satisfied to hear a strong, steady whirring.

"That's it. As good as new," he said.

Philippa thanked him and he went off on his ride. After the long, nervous drive in the solar car, he needed to work the kinks out of his system.

But his mind refused to cooperate. There was something, something he'd seen or something he'd heard at Philippa's that had made him uneasy, a feeling that he was missing something important.

He was back in the complex, riding past the habitation module when it hit him.

*Of course.*

He stopped suddenly, left his bike where it fell and entered the coral-like building. He rushed through the veins of stone that made up the interior of the apartment structure and stopped at the directory. The rooms he was looking for were located on the third floor.

Too impatient to wait for the elevator, Yevgeny sprinted up the steps three at a time. As soon as he located the door, he pounded on it, not bothering to locate the buzzer.

Jennifer answered. Her surprise at finding him looking like he'd just biked for an hour in the heat and then run up the stairs quickly faded, to be replaced by an expression of alarm.

She stepped back, turned towards the kitchen and took three steps forward. She tore open a drawer and reached inside.

"Don't," he said.

She stopped and looked back at him.

"Unless you have a gun stashed in there, you won't be able to get rid of me. I grew up in Russia in the Transition. The first thing we learned as kids was how to defend ourselves against someone with a knife. I don't want to have to break your arm."

Jennifer glared at him.

"Besides," he continued. "What are you hoping to gain? A couple of hours? Someone will notice I'm missing.

Someone will remember me coming in here. They'll find you soon enough. It's over."

And then she broke down, sat cross-legged on the floor still clutching the knife, and cried.

• • •

The two pieces of technology were, as Yevgeny had expected, long gone, but a couple of folders in the apartment turned up blueprints of things still in the works. They were things that Jennifer should never have had access to. Things that she must have taken off the director's desk.

Siti sat down facing her.

"You have no right to violate my privacy this way," Jennifer said, pretending anger. It was obvious, however, that she was actually scared and frightened.

"The folders were on the table. We haven't even searched for anything else. You should let go of the knife."

Jennifer looked at it as if she'd forgotten it was in her hand. She dropped it onto the floor and pushed it away.

"Thank you." Siti gave her a hard look. "Do you want to tell me who you were working for?"

"Would it make any difference?"

"Not really. I won't let you stay no matter who it was."

Jennifer's tears exploded from her once again. Yevgeny's heart broke. He knew the woman had been there for years. Even though she'd been caught red-handed, he was sure the emotion was genuine.

"Is it a corporation?"

Jennifer's sadness disappeared, to be replaced by rage, but

it passed quickly. Defeat was the only thing she had left. "What do you take me for?"

"I took you for a loyal member of the community. Now ... you tell me."

"I'm going to miss this place. You. Everything. I really do believe. But so many people don't."

"Oh." Siti sounded sad.

It suddenly became clear to Yevgeny that Jennifer must be part of one of the many fringe groups determined to force their lifestyle on people who weren't ready for it, or even particularly interested.

"I'll just pack, then," Jennifer said.

"Yes." Siti turned to go, but stopped. "Wait. Before you go, I have a message for your ... people."

"What?" There was defiance in Jennifer's features now. She knew that no one would hurt her. No one would keep her from leaving. That wasn't the way they did things there.

"Tell them that I'm willing to share everything we're doing here. Both what's already been done and what we're developing. I'll give them as much as the lab can produce. But I have one condition. They have to live here for a year, and see if they can't learn from our methods as well. Maybe if they learn how to teach instead of how to dictate, people will listen to them. Tell them to send an emissary. Two or even ten if they want. You know we can feed as many as they can send." Siti's features hardened. "We'll accept anyone but you."

Now Siti did walk out. Yevgeny followed her; there

wasn't really anything for him to do in Jennifer's apartment. He'd already done enough damage.

Out on the path, Siti allowed him to catch up. The woman's stride was much too long for him, and he wasn't going to run after her.

"How did you know?" she said.

"The day we were late for lunch … she pretended she'd been working late. I knew you'd never let that happen. But I only realized it today."

"You're smarter than you look. Are you sure you don't want to go to work in the lab? The offer is still open, you know. I know Hermes says he can use you. And I'm sure you can optimize the drone electronics if they give you access to the codes. I've been having trouble keeping them as steady as I'd like."

"No thanks. I'm all right," he replied.

• • •

Two days later, he took a day off. The drone recharging field had been a harder job than he imagined. There'd been a short-circuit somewhere, and it had taken him hours to track it to a cracked cable casing inside the complex itself. But it was done, and drones had been taking off and landing all day. He'd even seen the cooling mesh grid—the element that would, in theory, condense the water in the air—fly at one point. It was as big as a football field, but light enough that the drones could lift it and maneuver.

He chuckled. Siti was doing excellent work, but her obsession for controlling the weather would lead nowhere.

Oscar and Philippa, two of the great minds of humanity, had beaten their heads against the problem for forty years and never gotten around it. Siti's approach was a bit different, but it depended on too many variables to work. He just hoped the obsession didn't distract her from more fruitful pursuits.

Of course, he could never tell her that directly. The closest he could ever come was to joke with her about it and hope she took the hint.

Even on his days off, the bike ride was sacred. He mounted at exactly six. There was still an hour left until sundown, and he saw that his hopes of Siti relaxing her urge to control the rain were in vain. She was still at it.

The drones, complete with condenser grid, lifted from the charging field as soon as he rode out of the complex.

The formation appeared tight enough, with each drone holding its position. Hermes must have rewritten the algorithms.

He watched until the individual drones were almost invisible in the sky, then set his eyes back to the road.

Fifteen minutes into his ride, a drop fell on his head. Then another.

Yevgeny looked around. There wasn't a cloud in the sky. *Incredible ... Siti's rig was working.*

But that couldn't be. She'd said she needed weeks of testing before she would turn it on.

And yet, another look into the sky confirmed it was the only possible explanation. Not one cloud. And now it was raining steadily enough to be annoying.

Well, at least he'd ride out of it in a hundred metres or so. The net wasn't all that big.

Forty-five minutes later, he came to a stop in front of his workshop, soaked to the skin. It had rained on him the entire way.

Siti was waiting for him, her face expressionless.

"You made it rain on me all the way," he said.

"Yes," she replied.

"That was …"

Siti finally couldn't control herself any longer and burst out laughing. "It was what you deserved. That was what it was. You never believed."

He was about to retort, but caught himself and lowered his eyes. "No. I didn't."

"Do you believe now?"

"Do I have any choice? The impossible can happen."

"Yes. It can."

Was that an opening? No. It couldn't be.

But if it was, he would never forgive himself. "You owe me dinner for this," he said.

"No. Not dinner. Dinner is a communal affair. You know that." His heart sank. Just like that, in a second, she'd shot him down.

She let the silence continue for another two heartbeats, and then she smiled. "But if you can get your hands on a bottle of something, I'd be up for a few drinks on the lab terrace afterwards."

"I thought the lab closed after dark."

Her smile broadened. "I have a key."

He watched her walk off, admiring, as he always did, her perfectly straight posture. Then he snapped out of it. Dinner was in twenty minutes. He needed to change out of the wet clothes ... and where in the world was he going to get a bottle of anything good on such short notice?

Yevgeny sprang into motion.

# ABOUT THE AUTHOR

Gustavo Bondoni is a novelist and short story writer with over four hundred stories published in fifteen countries, in seven languages. He is a member of Codex and a Full Member of SFWA. He has published six science fiction novels including one trilogy, four monster books, a dark military fantasy and a thriller. His short fiction is collected in *Pale Reflection* (2020), *Off the Beaten Path* (2019), *Tenth Orbit and Other Faraway Places* (2010) and *Virtuoso and Other Stories* (2011).

In 2019, Gustavo was awarded second place in the Jim Baen Memorial Contest and in 2018 he received a Judges Commendation (and second place) in The James White Award. He was also a 2019 finalist in the Writers of the Future Contest.

His website is at www.gustavobondoni.com.

# THE BRIGHTER WORLD

## Robert Dawson

THE sun was so hot, and the two full wooden buckets weighed so much! No matter how Tallie held them, their hard handles, salvaged Old-Time wire wrapped in rawhide, hurt her fingers or her palms, and every time she stepped carelessly, another gout of the precious water would slop out into the dust and filth of the street. But big sister Hepsa needed the water so she could have supper ready when Mother and Father came home hungry and tired from the fields, and fetching it was Tallie's job.

In some places, the villagers built long conduits out of adze-hollowed logs, or even out of stone, to bring fresh water in. Traders sometimes had lengths of Old-Time pipe, too, closed and perfectly round, made of copper or strange slippery stuff called plastic. The village smith liked the copper, and the plastic tube made good spouts: but the pieces were far too short for a conduit, and nobody knew the secret of joining them anymore.

Tallie scuffed viciously at a pebble, careful not to let her shoulders join in the motion. She knew how to use an adze, at least for simple jobs, but building a conduit all the way from the spring to the village was far too much work for one little girl. It figured: the workers who were good at building things weren't the ones who had to carry the water. Grownups said that the work built character, but grownups always said silly things like that. Tallie was doing perfectly well with the character she had now. And ... the buckets were so heavy.

She was at the marketplace now: only a little way to go before she was home and could put the buckets down. Hepsa would still want her to peel vegetables and sweep the floor, but that wasn't so bad.

Today wasn't market day: the square was empty except for one thin grey-haired woman, a stranger, slouching on one of the hewn-log benches. She wore a shirt of coarse woven stuff, and a worn deerskin skirt. A battered walking stick rested against her legs, the wood grimy with long use. When the woman saw Tallie, she pulled herself up straighter. "Come here, girl," she said. "I want to tell you a story."

"I've got to get home, aunt," said Tallie.

The woman reached into her patched leather shoulder pouch. "Would you like this apple?"

Tallie looked dubiously at the small wrinkled fruit. The village storerooms had better, though at this time of year, early summer, they were only given out once a week. How could she refuse politely? Sharp eyes watched her expression.

"You've been working so hard, dear, carrying those big buckets for your family. You deserve a little rest and a bite to eat."

Tallie couldn't argue with that. She set the buckets down and held out her hand. "That's very kind of you, aunt."

The old woman smiled and gave her the apple, then began like all the storytellers did. "Hear me!" Her voice rose in the traditional chant, pitched to attract an audience out of a noisy market-day crowd. It sounded strange in the empty square. "Hear me! Hear me, and I'll tell you a tale, a tale of long ago and far away."

"Do you know any stories about werewolves? Or spaceships?" Tallie took a bite from the apple. The flesh was no longer crisp, but there was only one small rotten patch.

"Yes, I do, but they aren't the story you're going to hear now." The woman was using her normal voice again. "I'm going to tell you a story of how people began to work together."

Once a crowd had put a few coins into a storyteller's cup, they usually wrangled amongst themselves about the choice of story: that was the first part of the entertainment, and could go on for some time. But today, Tallie was eating the storyteller's apple, and it wasn't her place to argue. She nodded. "The adults work together in our fields every day. Some days we work with them."

"*This is different.*" Sharp iron in the woman's voice. "This is a story of the years when the seas began to rise. When the sun burned the plants, and the winds scoured the soil. This is the story of what people did to save the world."

"Tell me, please." Tallie flicked the rotten bit of the apple into the dust with her thumbnail, took another bite, and made herself comfortable at the empty end of the bench.

"In those years a leader came forth. She had a voice that could charm a baby from its mother's breast, that could talk a squirrel down from a tree, or soothe the storm wind. She saw that the earth was sick, sick from the breath of the factories and the machines. She saw that the storms grew worse each year, and that the seas rose higher. For years she had watched the earth grow sicker, waiting for somebody to take the lead and fix things: and when nobody else stepped forward, she did so herself. She called people together—first the people from her town, then from her country, and finally from the whole big round world—and she told them that they were dancing down the road to destruction." The storyteller paused.

At this point, usually some grownup would have added another coin to the cup, but Tallie had none. "Did they listen to her?" she asked.

"How could they do otherwise? I tell you, child, she had a voice of gold. And she was not alone: she gathered helpers around her. There were wise scientists who knew all the secrets of nature, and clever engineers who could build anything you could think of. There were administrators who could turn a thousand aimless people into an efficient team, and financiers who could find the money to pay for it all."

Tallie wasn't sure quite what all these people did, but it

sounded very grand and wonderful. She hugged herself and listened.

The old storyteller's eyes glittered. "She told the people that it was too late to save some of their cities, but that they could save the rest—and they listened to her, and they built new homes for those whose old homes were lost. She told them that if those who had more than they needed helped those who had lost everything, then everybody would have something—and the rich people heard her, and they gave, and they gave. No longer was it the fashion to be wasteful while others went hungry and homeless. And she told the people of the world that they could be strong and brave, and that they could choose the way of honour—and those who had once been weak and fearful became such a force for good as the world has never known. They faced hardship gladly; they worked beside old enemies like sisters and brothers; and in the end they won through, and the new world that they built together was brighter and better than before."

Tallie popped the core in her mouth and chewed. She looked around at the dusty marketplace, at the shacks lining the stinking road. People said that the Old-Time world had been a place of marvels, of buildings a thousand feet high, of machines that flew like birds and ran faster than horses. If there was a world even brighter than that, it must be somewhere very far away! Anyhow, the apple and the story were finished. She stood up, reached to take up her buckets again, then remembered her manners. "Are you thirsty, aunt?" Carefully, so as not to spill any water, she moved one of the buckets over by the woman's feet, putting it within easy reach.

The woman smiled. "I am, dear! Telling stories is thirsty work." She took a tin mug from her pouch, reached down, dipped up water still cold from the spring, and sipped. "Thank you very much."

Tallie looked at the stranger's lined face, her tight lips, and sensed an untold secret. "Aunt, is that a true story?"

The storyteller gazed silently into the depths of her tin mug. "It's a story," she said.

Tallie hesitated. "Were you once that woman, the leader?"

"Weren't you listening, child?" She slapped the bench, impatiently. "I told you it was just a story! We had no leaders —no real leaders. That was the problem! And me? In university I presented a few papers about climate change to people who already agreed with what I said." Tallie had only a vague idea what a university was, but the old woman's voice was so bitter and so intense that she was afraid to interrupt. "Then I went into politics, because they said that was the best way to become powerful. Like all the other politicians, I told people that they could have whatever they wanted—maybe not right now, but very soon. And I was good at telling them that—oh, I was very, very good." She sighed. "But we all knew that the world was going to hell, didn't we? And we all looked the other way because it was easier. And so, of course, it happened. Maybe we—maybe I—could have done more. We'll never know, will we?"

Tallie's eyes prickled with tears. She blinked them away, bit her lip. "Then … then why tell me that stupid story, if it's not true?" Instantly she regretted her rudeness, but the old woman's expression did not change.

"Because every story's a lesson, child. And every lesson's a possibility." She put her cup away and got to her feet, straightening as stiffly as a rusty hinge, using her stick to lever herself upward. "Thank you for the water."

"Have you eaten, aunt?" Tallie asked. Hepsa would grumble later in private about not being warned, but hospitality to travellers was everybody's obligation.

The woman shook her head. "There's somewhere else I have to get to tonight. But it's good of you to ask, dear. Now remember that story, and when your chance comes to make this poor world a better place—*do it!*" She flashed a quick grin, then turned and walked, with only a hint of a limp, toward the big road that led to the next village and the wide world beyond.

Tallie picked up her heavy buckets and trudged homeward. That water conduit, now: *that* was something that would make the world a better place. The village, anyway. But she'd have to get a lot of other people to help her build it … and that would mean standing up at the next village meeting, making her proposal in front of all the adults and elders, and explaining why it was so important. The thought made her feel trembly inside, but she knew that she could do it.

And then maybe they could all do something about the stinky streets.

# ABOUT THE AUTHOR

Robert Dawson teaches mathematics at a Nova Scotian university. His stories have appeared in *Nature: Futures*, *AE*, and numerous other periodicals and anthologies. He's an alumnus of the Sage Hill and Viable Paradise writing workshops.

# SHIPWRECKED EARTH
## Wade Thiel

YOU look to me
With bloodshot eyes.
You look to me
Through opaque, plastic lenses
For help,
But I can't help
But feel helpless.
I can't help
But try, fearing
You are doomed.
I fear my help
Won't make difference enough,
No matter how hard I try,
And so I pick up
The broken pieces of you
And make a garden
In my own yard.

The wind blows dust
In waves like swelling seawater,
And you, the shipwrecked earth,
Slip silently into the depths.

# ABOUT THE AUTHOR

Wade Thiel is a writer who lives in Indianapolis, Indiana. His journalism has appeared in various publications including, *Outdoor Life Magazine*, *Money*, *RV Magazine*, *Web Bike World*, and others. His fiction and poetry have appeared in the *Tipton Poetry Review*, *Etchings*, *Polk Street Review*, *The Good Men Project*, and elsewhere. You can reach him at www.wadethiel.com.

# THINGS WE DO BEFORE WE EAT

## Jason P. Burnham

DANNY loved Central Park. Danny's father, Thomas, hated the walk through the pencil towers that got them there.

"Can we please do a boat ride today, Daddy?"

"Sure, buddy." Thomas scanned the sidewalks ahead of him, trying to pick out any areas where they might run across someone Thomas didn't want to have to explain to Danny.

Danny stopped short and looked back at Thomas. "Maybe we can have a snack on the boat?" he asked hopefully.

Thomas sighed. He was on edge from meandering through the towers and another request for snacks wasn't helping his nerves. A stiff could pop out of an entryway or hidden exit at any moment.

"Did you bring the peanut butter crackers?" Danny

asked, piling on. What else did a five-year-old have to worry about besides food?

"We've not helped anyone yet today. If you want to eat on the boat, let's find someone to help."

Danny wrinkled up his nose into a pout. He wanted crackers; not to have to help someone. Then suddenly, he smiled.

"How about that man?" Danny pointed at a disheveled, cachectic man in the shadow of the overhang of the nearest pencil tower.

Thomas recoiled. *Dammit.* Sometimes they made it to Central Park without encountering any stiffs. They preferred their penthouses to being seen out in public, but occasionally they did have to come down and interact with others. He supposed they got hungry too, even if they wouldn't admit it.

"It's not polite to point," said the man in shadow. He had a day's worth of black stubble, which stood taller against his sunken face. His charcoal suit hung from his pale white frame like it was on a plastic hanger. Thomas could practically see the outlines of his ribs through the suit. The man held a cigarette to his lips. Some of the stiffs used nicotine to suppress hunger.

"Come along, Danny," Thomas guided Danny by putting his hand on top of his head.

"But Daddy!" Danny stomped his feet. "That man looks *so hungry.*" Danny quieted and scrunched up his face, as if making a very hard decision. "I think …" He started to whisper. "I think we might have to give him our crackers."

There was a raspy cough from behind them, a smoker's chuckle. "Kid, I don't want your stupid crackers. Move along, why don't you?"

"That was very nice of you, Danny," Thomas reassured him. He grabbed Danny's warm little hand and led him to the park.

Danny was quiet until they reached the tree line, then he stopped and looked back toward the pencil towers.

"Why'd that man use a bad word, Daddy? Why was he so grumpy? Was it 'cause he was so hungry?"

Thomas took a deep breath in and let it out. "You know how we have to help other people so our bodies will let us eat?"

Danny nodded fervently.

"Some people would rather not eat than do nice things for other people. I think that man doesn't want to do nice things for other people."

Danny cocked his head. "But why, Daddy? Doesn't he know how good peanut butter crackers are?"

Thomas couldn't help but smile. He nudged Danny forward and they continued walking toward the lake.

"When you were just a tiny baby, people put something in the water that, after we drank it, made it so our bodies couldn't digest food if we didn't help other people first. It made a lot of things better because everyone was helping not only each other, but animals, the land, the oceans, the *whole planet*. But some people didn't want the world to change. They didn't want to do nice things. So now they do the fewest nice things they can just to survive."

Danny considered this. "What happens if you don't do *any* nice things?"

"Then you die." Thomas said. When Danny frowned uncertainly, Thomas continued. "And *no* peanut butter crackers."

Danny gasped. "Who would want to live without peanut butter crackers?"

Thomas shrugged. "Beats me, buddy." He didn't bother to correct Danny's misunderstanding of the finality of death—an anticipated paucity of peanut butter crackers conveniently conveyed the direness of the situation.

They arrived at the placid lake and climbed onto a rowboat after putting on their orange life vests.

"Would you like your crackers now?" Thomas asked.

Danny's eyes went wide. "But I didn't do anything nice, Daddy. I don't want to throw them up."

Thomas pulled the crackers out of his backpack and handed one to Danny. "You were nice to offer that man your crackers even though he was mean and told us to go away. I think that was nice enough for some crackers."

Danny took the cracker from Thomas's hand and tentatively put it to his lips. When he didn't throw up the first bite, he relaxed and ate them ravenously, crumbs spilling into the bottom of the boat.

When he was done, Danny took a big gulp of water and handed the bottle back.

"Daddy?"

"Yeah, bud?"

"Even though he said no, I think we should still keep trying to be nice. Maybe that man will change his mind and be nice too."

Thomas smiled. He loved the optimism of youth.

"Maybe so, buddy. We'll keep trying."

# ABOUT THE AUTHOR

Jason P. Burnham loves spending time with his wife, kids, and dog. He strives to do his small part in the collective actions necessary to ensure the things he loves have a planet that remains habitable for them. He also coedits *If There's Anyone Left,* a magazine of inclusive speculative fiction with his friend C. M. Fields.

# ONE LAST BASH BEFORE WE ALL HIT THE ROAD

## Louis Evans

THE Ball at the End of the World existed at that narrow intersection of refined taste, decadent excess, and ironic misanthropy where all truly daring social coups occur.

Of course it was Salvatore Arravanche's idea.

And because it was an Arravanche event, everyone came. There were no invitations—no illuminated scraps of cardstock, no cloying notifications ricocheting madly from phone to phone. Arravanche never bothered with such banalities as invitations. Everyone who was anyone always showed up anyway.

And it wasn't any different for the Ball at the End of the World.

And we came.

Even while Hurricane Naomi bore down upon

Manhattan, no more than eighteen hours off and still gaining power, even as she ratcheted up into that hazy space between Category 8 and Category 9, the same strength Marcus and Chantelle and Patricia had been when they'd wiped Florida, DC, and the Carolinas off the map, we came.

Even though northbound Routes 87 and 95 trickled, filled, and then glutted bumper to bumper with SUVs and minivans and overstuffed sedans packed three four five six seven to a car, cherished possessions lashed to the roof, pets held in laps, the same climate refugee caravan that we'd seen abandon a dozen great metropolises already, we came.

Even as the trains ran emergency service from South Ferry north to Mt. Vernon, packed beyond capacity by no more than a few stations past departure, as on foot the huddled masses surged over bridges, finding higher ground, even as the mayor stood at City Hall in the rising wind and spoke in a voice like the granite bedrock of the island, saying simply "do not attempt to stay,"—we came to the party.

Even as everyone who was no one fled the city, everyone who was anyone came. Some rode chauffeured limos and faux self-driving cars. These days they are a scam; the desert is too hot for data centers anymore, and hidden in the trunk a man drives by camera. Some of us flew in by helicopter, whirling back down from our retreats in the Berkshires. A handful arrived by submarine—a nuclear missile boat converted to a luxury redoubt for a dozen persons of means, whose captain would submerge her into the Hudson canyon when Naomi hit and ride out the storm a quarter-mile beneath the waves, and whose passengers insisted that it resurface so they could make it to the last party of all the parties. Just a couple came on foot: at any Manhattan party there are always those lucky few who happen to live a single block over, for whom any other mode of transit is an affectation.

And I came by subway.

It is common knowledge that in New York City everyone, rich or poor, takes the subway. It's mostly true, which is to say, true enough. As I waited for the elevator, smoothing my lapels and evening out the wings of my bowtie, it occurred to me: this would be my last chance to ride. I cancelled my car as I descended toward the lobby. Our doormen had long since deserted their posts and so I let myself out into the street.

I went underground at Canal Street. Two minutes until the Q; I spent them idly regarding the subway map. So many different places to go, even with the ugly NO SERVICE bruise that had covered the South Brooklyn from Red Hook to Coney Island ever since Hurricane Simon four years back. So many things I'd never get the chance to do.

In life you always have all the time in the world right up until there's no time left at all.

The Q pulled into the station and I rode it uptown. The Q is not an evacuation route—it never leaves the island of Manhattan—and so the crowd of riders was almost preternaturally ordinary. Commuters headed home. Revellers headed out. Homeless headed nowhere. One old guy sat in a heap of shopping bags—two dozen, three dozen—clearly the result of a hunkering-down grocery run. Maybe he hadn't heard the mayor's warning. Maybe he had never seen the pictures of downtown Miami after Marcus, towers sheared and twisted, of Washington after Chantelle returned it overnight to the swamp. Maybe he just didn't care.

Nobody tried to warn him. In a disaster it would be different but on the normal subway you don't talk to strangers, and Naomi had not yet made landfall.

At Midtown I got off the train. When I emerged from underground, the scene was gratifyingly distressed. Traffic in the escape-bound directions—uptown to the Bronx or west to Jersey—had the appropriate rags-and-tatters refugee aesthetic, as reconceived in a city where everyone wears black and my pants cost more than you make in a year. Pedestrians on foot with heavy bags coursed in the same directions. New York is always bustling but this was something more; the only person staying in one spot was a homeless man leaning against the edge of a building. His cup overflowed with spare bills he would not have a chance to spend.

The party was in the ballroom of a certain grand hotel. Unlike our apartment building, Arravanche had held on to his doormen. They were out of their customary livery and instead dressed in turquoise and aquamarine formalwear; each wore a half-facemask in the pattern of a beachdrift skull. though which half—brow or jaw, or left or right profile—varied from servant to servant. Arravanche must have bought out the whole building. He was always doing shit like that.

As I neared the door, I saw two doormen turn away an insistent woman in an evening gown. She must have known about the party, and normally that was all one needed to enter an Arravanche event, but this time a stricter list was clearly being enforced. Good for them; as she stomped off past me, improbably high heels entwining like ruched and sparkling seaweed around her calves, I recognized Lucia Cortez, gossip blogger and mocker, muckraker, and hot-taker. An "activist."

Good riddance. The last party she'd managed to crash was poor Ronnie Wackym's birthday and in the quiet lull between the appetizers and the entrées she had climbed onto a table, a cell phone recording in each hand, and asked us all how we could eat molecular gastronomy while the DC refugees starved in the Hoboken camps.

I approached the doormen. Up close their masks went from daring to genuinely uncanny. Glass eyes set in sand-bleached bone—a facsimile, I had to assume—stared silently at me for longer than was comfortable. But whatever list Lucia was off, I was on, and they waved me inside.

When you grow up in Manhattan's upper crust the layout of certain Midtown hotels is seared into your marrow by countless childhood excursions. Arravanche had erected false walls, movable screens, and drop cloths; the familiar layout had been reinscribed with a foreign labyrinth, on whose walls were painted waves, aquatic scenes, maps of the city, plans for failed skyscrapers. Still I made it through, step by twisting step, and until I quite suddenly found myself in the ballroom.

This was where Arravanche's genius made itself known.

In truth, any party on that night would have been a smashing success, if only because there were no other parties to attend. But Arravanche was not content with success; he insisted upon mastery.

The ballroom was, as always, cavernous. Its eaves were darkened and angled mirrors gave it the depth of the night sky. Pinprick LEDs suggested stars, and the flash of floodlights gave us the lightning outside. The food lined the east and west walls of the ballroom. And what a feast! Calving icebergs of crystal sugar. Chocolate landslides a story high. Charleston red rice in little waterproof dishes sunken beneath a saltwater lake. Churrascaria in the shape of rescue helicopters. Punch bowls of morir soñando with swirling hurricanes of foam. The ¡Cuba Aquae!, a cocktail of gin and club soda and just a hint of sugarcane. Ice sculptures of nudes from classical antiquity, staged half-melted. And on and on ...

And in the center of the ballroom was the coup de grâce: the dance floor.

The entire dance floor had been remade into a map of the city. The only true city that is; the island of Manhattan. That familiar shape, a fumble-fingered hand-rolled cigarette, a butcher's knife, rose embossed in mahogany from the floor. The map, Midtown's regular grid and its damaged daughters—Heights, Village, Battery, their streets askew—was picked out in subtle inlays of oak and cherry. And the pièce de résistance: in the Hudson and East Rivers, in the Harlem River and the Spuyten Duyvil, carved into the floor, there were actual rivers of water flowing from the north end of the ballroom out to the harbour in the south. Just an inch deep, but still. It was incredible.

I did not show my surprise. New York was a Dutch city first, and an English one after that; our upper classes have always carried an emotional reserve with them. One doesn't gasp, ever. But I was impressed.

The ballroom filled. I nibbled on a Miami-style fish taco, garnished with saltwater and forget-me-nots. Once the cod would have been too low-class to make an appearance at a meal like that, but these days fish are worth their weight in gold.

It was delicious regardless.

It was still in that early state of the party where you talk to your acquaintances; not your friends. I went swirling through the preparty motions. Seeing and being seen. Exchanging a nod or just a few words. We seldom touched on the important, or even the novel. When we spoke of the dance floor we did so in studied, worldly tones. Nobody mentioned Hurricane Naomi.

When everyone who was anyone had finally sussed out their way to the ballroom, the lights blackened, then flashed. The faux thunder roared.

Everyone was glancing around, stifling their excitement, hiding their fear; waiting for Arravanche to make his entrance.

When he did it was, gratifyingly, as grand as I'd hoped. The lights darkened for almost a minute and then a single spotlight sliced through the darkness and fell upon the middle of Manhattan—but instead of flat wood there was an imposing, ten-foot model of the Empire State Building. It was cartoonishly out of proportion, squat and stubby, but the distorted shape was unmistakable. It looked something like those rubbery tchotchkes that tourists buy at JFK and LaGuardia and that they would now install in their makeshift climate shrines in their hometowns all over the country. Which would eventually be themselves abandoned as the lines of heat and storm marched inexorably up the map.

Straddling the tall mast with his feet firmly planted on the exaggeratedly broad observation deck, which widened into a sort of grotesque podium, was Salvatore Arranche.

He was clad in a resplendent suit of shimmering rainbow scales. On anyone else it would have seemed like an entertainer's affectation but on him it was somehow the height of fashion. His shoes were black. His tie was black. His eyeshadow was sparkling.

He swung easily around the antenna and for one absurd moment I was confident he would burst into that old Gene Kelly number, "I'm singin' in the rain! Just singin' in the rain ..."

But camp was never quite his style. Instead he remained standing upright. His smile somehow widened.

"Welcome, friends!"

Scattered polite applause.

"Tonight is the very last night of the city of New York."

A deeply awkward silence. It was true. We all knew it was true. The truth was etched into the Weather Channel maps and the refugee caravans and the discreet, unequivocal presentations we had each received from our family's wealth managers. The truth was etched into our faces and our feet and our spines. A truth like this was not for saying.

But Salvatore Arranche said it. That was the kind of man he was. And awkward or not he kept speaking.

"Tonight is the very last bite of the big apple, the final crowning glory in the Empire city, the ultimate twirl at the very center of the universe.

"But, friends, we are not going gentle into that good night! We greet the final storm not with a mewling whimper but with pyrotechnics, with the biggest bang of them all! I have sealed this storied hotel against all intruders! Here in this exclusive paradise we are safe from the chaos outside. Here we can show *Naomi* that New York society is not afraid of anything!

"My friends, welcome to the Ball at the End of the World!"

His hands erupted in a flourish. Mad applause erupted from the crowd; hoots and cheers. Doors at the periphery of the ballroom flung open and servants rushed in with new carts, revealing that the lavish spread we'd seen was just the beginning. Haute cuisine and cheap street food. Halal Brothers and Joe's Pizza rubbed shoulders with Per Se and Momofuku. Cart upon cart upon cart of champagne, liquor, blow, pills, poppers—what would the NYPD do, *arrest* us?—tumbled inward. The music began to blare. Hidden screens descended and strobelights leapt to life. This was like no ball that had ever been.

I would like to say that we hesitated for a moment before throwing ourselves into debauchery. The truth is that everything happened instantaneously. From the first moment the first waiter, dashing theatrically, wheeled in the first mountain of cocaine, white powder streaming out behind him like the chemtrails from cloud-seeding jets that had not saved DC, we fell upon the feast like animals.

No. Not like animals. Like men.

What is there to say about the party? Well, what is there to say about any party? Light, noise, thirst. Gratification. I danced, gorged, fucked—I think, who's to say?—lay on the floor and howled, linked arms and sang, waltzed, fell over, watched a fistfight (encouraged it), washed out the loser's cuts with thousand-dollar vodka, set a small fire using hors d'oeuvres, snorted heroin off of a countess's "topless decolletage," that is, her tits.

Party stuff.

In a lull in the action I found myself over to the side, nibbling on a collapsed skyscraper made mainly of marzipan, and in that moment, by chance, by the swirling eddies of the party, my circle came to me. Parties are always doing that sort of thing; there's a magic to it.

There are basically three levels of social organization. The first is "society," which contains literally everyone you might conceivably want to know—old money and new, movie stars and magnates, artists and bankers, the whole shebang. Within society is the "crowd;" the sort of loose affiliation one belongs to. A crowd can be an age, or a place, or a club, or a hobby. And within the crowd is the "circle"—the people you actually do things with, all together.

There were five of us in my circle—me, and David, and Auvaline, and Michal, and Marguerie—and by that subtle party magic all of us were passing by the collapsed skyscraper at the same time and so of course we fell in together. Hugs all around, and kisses for the girls. Auvaline and I shared a look but didn't let it get beyond that. Whatever she'd been to me and I to her, we had the circle dynamic to consider.

Small talk ensued, desperately quotidien. I scanned the outfits. Marguerie in a fitted dress of coral silk, side-slit up to her hip, and Auvaline in a velvet sea-glass-green evening gown; David and Michal in assembly-line tuxedos. It was unlike Michal; he was always more fashionable than the rest of us and the Ball was certainly an opportunity to take a style risk.

"I know," he said, sorrowfully. "But all my good suits are already in Toronto."

"Is that where you're headed, then?" With the subject broached, I could finally ask what we'd all been wondering— where would we each be in the morning.

Michal nodded. "It's really the only great city left. The only one with true culture. I—"

"Well I'm going to Oslo," said Marguerie. It was of course quite like her to interrupt, but I didn't mind. "Half the clubs in the world are there now."

"Moscow for me," said David. "We're moving most of

the family business to Russia. They've got the land, and with all those Bangladeshi refugees they've got the manpower too. But if you work in Russia you have to live in Moscow." He shrugged. "It's not so bad."

"Daddy's dragging the whole family to that compound he bought up in Alberta," said Auvaline. Frowns around the circle. "I know, I know. But it's just until things settle down, he says."

Four pairs of eyes turned to me.

"Oh, I don't know," I said. "The Adirondacks, for now."

Marguerie laughed. "Oh, come on."

"Be realistic," said David. "The Adirondacks aren't a place, they're a, a *suburb*. The city's going away. You can't come back."

And then it was said and there was no going back from that either.

A long pause. Out on the dance floor the music beat out its endless crescendo.

"It's a damn shame," said Auvaline. "A damn shame." She sounded almost angry, which was quite a lot of sentiment for her. I've never known Auvaline to let her feelings show. Even in those two wondrous weeks we spent secretly engaged in Paris, when I wept with joy or sorrow she would never do more than wryly shrug.

Nods around the circle. "Someone should have done something," said David, forcefully, decisively. More nods, and mine among them, for who can disagree with that? Someone *should* have done something. Something *should* have been done.

But I couldn't help but remember that David's family money was in energy, which is to say coal and gas, which is to say: carbon dioxide. That Michal's father had bought and sold banks for the Saudi royal family—most of whom, these days, are no longer in their now-dessicated and ungovernable kingdom, but living peacefully in compounds along the Humber River, not far from Toronto. That Marguerie's money came from everywhere and nowhere, but that her mother's chequebook had never been closed when the right sort of lobbyist came calling to beat back government overreach and creeping socialism in environmental regulation. That Auvaline was older money than any of us; that it all flowed down from a founding share of Standard Oil.

I tell these tales together and they sound like an accusation, like this is all *our* fault. But you must understand: these were my friends from childhood. These were just ordinary facts about their lives. Where does your father work. What does your mother do.

Someone should have done something.

And me?

Well. The family fortune is in a lot of places, which is a good idea when things are volatile. Much of it is these days in munitions, which is another way to monetize volatility. Drones and smartguns. Business is good.

Someone should certainly have done something.

But perhaps the vicious tenor of my thoughts passed unnoticed because Marguerie spoke then, and she said "If only we'd had someone like Salvatore Arravanche back then. *He* could have straightened it out."

"What are you talking about?" said David. "He's just a venture capitalist. Who, granted, throws great parties, but they had tons of venture capitalists back then."

"He's not a VC," said Michal. "I heard he just won the Turbo Trillions lottery. Twice."

The government has mostly ground to a halt but the lotteries are still running. We must have bread and roses, and, failing both, at least the whirling gold sign of the roulette wheel.

"No, he's a producer," said Marguerie.

"A producer's what you are when you *have* money," said David. "We're talking about how he *got* it."

"You can make your money in producing."

"Not Arravanche money."

"You never—"

"You always—"

"I heard," said Auvaline, with that quiet tone that always cut through the rest of our bickering, "that he's the man who sold Nauru."

"What?"

"Yeah," said Auvaline. "You know. Nauru? Pacific Island country? Completely flooded? Nothing to be done about it. Nothing left but refugees. And then some midlevel minister sold the country to an international consortium for tax purposes? And now everyone's yachts are under Nauru flag and you're all pretending to be Nauruan on your tax returns?"

Mingled looks of confusion and familiarity revealed who precisely in our circle was paying attention to their tax strategies, but I will not tell on my friends.

"Anyway," she continued. "I heard that he—the guy who sold Nauru—said that he would give the money to the refugees, you know? Set up orphanages, that sort of thing, since he had lost his own family in the floods. Or something. So everyone felt good about it. But then he took the cash and disappeared. Three years later up pops Arravanche. Different name, different face, but you can buy those. And that's the story."

"Shit," said Michal. "The big brass balls on the guy to pull something like that off! I'll drink to that!" His glass rose wobblily. Mine did not follow. Something about Auvaline's story filled me with a formless dread.

"Say," I said. "Has anyone seen Arravanche? In the past few hours?"

Headshakes around the circle.

"You know," said David, "for that matter. The waiters seem to have gone too."

So they had. The carts, so generously laden, stood empty where emptied, stood half-empty where half-emptied; the refuse, of all kinds, was everywhere. Nobody was cleaning it up.

"What time is it?" said David. "I think I'd actually better be off." We checked. It was quite a bit later than we had realized. Time flies when you're snorting lines of snow. You've got all the time in the world right up until there's none left at all.

Marguerie held in her scream long enough to fling herself at the nearest door and so she was the first to find that they were sealed and locked. Airtight. Answering screams from across the ballroom, barely audible above the mechanical music that still pounded out on the dance floor, suggested that she was not the only one to make that discovery.

David rushed up behind her, shoved her out of the way, and began to slam his shoulder into the door. Michal got a tray and started hammering on the knob. Marguerie fell to her knees behind them, crying.

And Auvaline, my love, stepped one foot closer to the spot where I still stood, rooted to the floor. In that voice of pure and lovely irony, just as light as if we were speaking of the weather, she asked me, "Does it feel a little ... warm to you?"

I nodded.

And then, of course, the water began to rise.

## ABOUT THE AUTHOR

Louis Evans grew up in a Manhattan high rise. (Where does your father work. What does your mother do.) He lives not far from rising waters. His work has appeared previously in *Little Blue Marble*, as well as in *Vice*, *F&SF*, *Nature: Futures*, and more.

# CATASTROPHIZING

## Katie McIvor

IT isn't always the water that frightens me. When the floods lap below George IV Bridge, the Old Town drowning beneath a surging tide of brownish green, I find the water itself quite beautiful, in a majestic sort of way. What scares me is the waste the water leaves behind. The sea salt that settles like snow on pavements and windowsills as the flood recedes. The wash-line of sickly scum up the sides of buildings. The dead rats, the crabs, the corpses.

I can't go down into the lower levels of the city anymore. Last time I tried was on an evening out with Càit, my flatmate. We sat in the starkly lit restaurant halfway up a narrow close and I watched the water swirl under the door, up the table legs, into the pockets of Càit's jacket draped over the chair. Eventually I had to tell her. I remember the way she peered at me, her confusion magnified by the thick lenses she wears. I've never told anybody else.

Our flat, thank god, is up a hill at the top of Pentland

Terrace. We got the bus back that night, cancelling our plans for the cinema. My teeth chattered as we sloshed through thigh-deep slurry out of the restaurant. At the top of the close I turned and could see the water lapping at the steps. Back at the flat, I explained everything to Càit: the things I see, the horror of knowing that nobody else can see them. I felt ashamed of myself. The evening was supposed to have been a very different conversation, the one I never quite manage to have with her.

Càit frowned and Googled. "Advanced climate anxiety," she said with willed firmness. "That's all it is. You can get help for it."

I call her now, as I sit with my back to the wall above the Grassmarket. I can hear the water slapping on the stones beneath me. Càit's voice is calmness, an anchor in the depths. She asks how bad it is. Bad, but not the worst, I tell her, and my voice shakes only a little.

The worst attack I've had was last summer, when Càit invited me to visit her parents on the little island where she grew up. That island was hell for me. Càit's parents smiling at us like ghosts through the pearly murk, their whole house underwater, the whole island. I knew I was going mad. I woke each morning with sand crusted on the sheets, limpets clinging to me, the stench of rock pools in my hair.

I remember sitting opposite Càit in the garden with water lapping our necks. Her hair swirled around her in the current as she told me in a small, determined voice of her diagnosis. That was the first time it occurred to me how beautiful she was. She was garlanded with seaweed, her eyes the colour of the waves, filtered like sunlight through glass.

It takes her ten minutes to get to George IV Bridge. By that time I've calmed down a bit, the flood receding, although I can still hear and smell it. Càit sits with me on the dirty pavement. Her hands adjust the beanie she's taken to wearing since she started her treatment. I've never told her, but I love how she looks now, love the way her skin flows up the back of her neck and up and over her skull like a perfectly fitted cap. When she tips her head back to laugh, tiny crinkles form over the bones.

My hands clench in my lap. How I feel for Càit, these days, feeds into my other anxieties. I have the constant sense of time running out, of the world ending, of something beautiful facing its last, most vulnerable hours. I take several short breaths.

"Where's the water now?" Càit asks.

In my head, I want to tell her. In my dysfunctional eyeballs. About four feet down in the slopping gutters of the Grassmarket.

Instead I say, "You know I love you, don't you?" and my heart pulses in a great wave of exhilaration while the waters sink back down the slope, leaving their seaweed streaks on the walls, their discharge of algae—gone, for now, although they'll come back, again and again, as they always do.

# ABOUT THE AUTHOR

Katie McIvor is a writer from the Scottish Borders. Her short fiction has appeared or is forthcoming in magazines such as *The Deadlands*, *Uncharted*, *Fusion Fragment*, and the Bram Stoker Award-nominated anthology *Mother: Tales of Love and Terror*, and her three-story collection is out now with Ram Eye Press. You can find her on Twitter at @_McKatie_ or on her website at katiemcivor.com.

# CHOOSE YOUR OWN EXTINCTION

## Mike Morgan


Hear us

scream beg

in terror in pain in silence

as we

choke vomit grieve rage

powerless impotent hearts breaking thoughts boiling judging you

because of the

ash death loss destruction

from the

wildfires droughts heat

ravaging killing

the only world we have.


And

do something

before those who erred before our children, blameless

die

# ABOUT THE AUTHOR

Mike Morgan was born in London, but not in any of the interesting parts. He moved to Japan at the age of thirty and lived there for many years. Nowadays, he's based in Iowa, and enjoys family life with his wife and two young children. If you like his writing, be sure to check out his website: PerpetualStateofMildPanic.wordpress.com.

# EXTINCTION MEMORIALS
## Christopher Mark Rose

I remember coming to the Korean War Veterans Memorial, in its place on the National Mall in Washington, D.C., arriving early in the day, glimpsing it first through fog— maybe that's not possible, given it was a high school class trip, but that's my memory. The statues there, you could so clearly read the emotions forged in their features. Fear, awe, concern, anger, confusion. A fitting tribute, a place to remember and mourn the dead and the living who fought, and who all lost something in that conflict.

And then, not long after, coming to the Vietnam War Memorial, feeling its full effect. Thousands of names, a solid wall of loss. Americans should be burdened by the weight of all those names, the assembled company there, but grateful that its architect, I. M. Pei, gave us this gift. I watched my father seeking out the names of old friends, carved there into the rock. That's part of my experience now too. I won't forget.

That giant, polished earthwork, and the naked gash of earth that frames it, help us to remember. But more, they provide not just a prompt for grieving, but a safe place for mourning. Mourning is a moment of real vulnerability. People mourning are unguarded. They can be bereft, abject.

Mourning is the hard emotional work we all should do, we all must do. A memorial is not an inert piece of landscaping—it's a psychically active site, a place where humans are transformed.

Now, take a walk with me, from the Vietnam Memorial, across the National Mall, into the Smithsonian Museum of Natural History, down some stairs, and see, in modest, dusty vitrines, the bones of a dodo, the taxidermied corpse of a passenger pigeon. Next to them, some scholastic-sounding explanatory text. By chance, I came across these things on that same day, in just this order.

What a poor, ineffectual memorial we have unintentionally created for these extinct species. Even less, for the thousands of other species entirely gone from the face of the earth since humanity began its march across it— species for whom there are no memorials. There's nowhere to go, nothing to see or touch. No place to leave a stone, a flower, a memento.

We should all be ashamed.

In truth, it was human action that brought these species to extinction. I think it's late, but essential, for us to create a place to memorialize those species made extinct, in whole or in part, by human hands.

We are all, to one extent or another, responsible. It's well beyond the point of any debate. The evidence is clear, the verdict has come in, the jury is unanimous.

The humans. It was us. We're the guilty ones. We did it.

And I think it's crucial to note that some of us are more culpable than others. Capitalism and colonialism have been, and still are, delivering power and consequence into the hands of a few men—it's always men—whose choices have been paramount in driving what will be called the Sixth Mass Extinction. The Anthropocene Extinction.

Back on the Mall, back at the monuments: I love the country I was born to, the people and ideas it is assembled from. And the purple mountain majesties, the fruited plain. And I concede that not all of its wars were just.

• • •

We can't plumb now the depth of the loss, or the shattering trauma of carrying the responsibility of having participated in the murder of an untold richness of species, and not even having a place to process these things. Not even to know or feel the extent of what is gone. Our children will feel this too. Every generation's burden becomes heavier.

Look into the faces of your kids and tell them that we have the pyramids for the pharaohs, memorials and special cemeteries for the war dead, but for the extinct species, nothing. A lacuna—a deliberate and obvious void. They see that.

Our kids are watching us. They are aware. They learn from us, not just from the self-exculpatory stories we contrive and the poses we strike, but from how we transform the world around us, and what we value enough to actually make an effort for.

I remember my paternal grandfather. Not in life, because my encounters with him in that state were, fortunately, few and brief. But my father and I flew home with his ashes, after he passed in his shabby houseboat in Florida. That place was, to my young eyes, a disturbing mess—I remember disorder and filth, golf clubs, a shotgun, bourbon, nude polaroids. But somehow, in death, his presence disturbed me more.

It wasn't that the urn full of his ashes remained up in the shelf at the top of our coat closet for years—after all, they were just ashes, right? It was the sense of lack, that there was no real place for him, and for us to mourn, to accuse, or even just to remember him. The houseboat was swiftly sold. His mess auctioned off. No one ever showed up in that coat closet to eulogize him or recount his life.

So too the Moa. The Aurochs. The Black Rhino. Tell them, tell them, that they will remain forever unmemorialized, forever unmourned. That there's no place to go to remember them, except, maybe, a few glass cases in a museum somewhere.

This is wrong. This is insufficient.

My father and my brother finally did, one steamy June day, dig a hole in the family burial plot, and put Grandfather Rose's ashes into the ground. There might have been a few words said then, the character of which I cannot report. I was several states away then. But I'm glad it finally happened.

If there's a place for my grandfather, scoundrel that he was, and for the people his life touched, then surely there should be a place for these extinct species, innocent of everything but getting in the way of humanity, of wishing to share the same resources, the same bounty we together inherited.

In a time when so much ephemeral information is now so readily available to us, a memorial is a durable marker saying that these people or creatures or events are significant. Recognition that they are important to us. That we remember. This would not be, in any way, "environmental justice," but it would be just.

It might also serve as a prompt to us to pursue better courses in our own time.

I'm not asking for much. No prominent location on the shining National Mall. No massive marble statues. It could be anywhere, though it would be good if it were somewhere quiet, natural, beautiful. It could be meadow, or forest. Probably, the less manicured and obviously premeditated, the better. And probably we should make sure it's a big plot, the way things are going.

Let artists each choose a species, and make somber, humane memorials for those that are now unreachable to us. There is no risk of ever running out of choices.

Do we even know their names? Stellar's sea cow. Labrador duck. Tasmanian wolf. St. Helena olive tree. Golden toad. Réunion giant tortoise. Great auk. Our ignorance is appalling.

We need—not they, but we need—a place to see and to remember them, a place to accept our participation, tacit or active.

A place to admit and feel our sorrow at what has happened, our trauma, our mounting loneliness as a species. A place to grieve what has been lost. A place to traverse our pain, and create from it a resolve never to let this happen again.

That's what memorials are.

# ABOUT THE AUTHOR

Christopher Mark Rose is a husband and father, an electrical engineer for NASA spacecraft, and in his spare time an author of speculative fictions. His writings have appeared in *Interzone* and *Dreamforge*, and are forthcoming in *Asimov's* and *UNCANNY*. He attended the most recent Viable Paradise writers' workshop, and is founder for the Charm City Spec reading series. He hopes his stories are affecting, humane, and concerned with large questions.

# THE PRAIRIE SCHOOL
## Christopher R. Muscato

IT'S all … lines.

Penny lowers her sketchbook and looks at her campfire. It flickers, catching the breeze. She looks back at her sketchbook. Lines. Lots of lines. A visual emphasis on the horizontal, intercut with organic motifs. Plans for off-grid, solar-powered tiny homes. Built from an architect's perspective. She flips through old pages, old sketches. Lines, but no connections. The designs aren't coming together, which seems fitting because what is? Paths, roads, options, choices, lines. Diverging. Not uniting. No clear direction.

Penny drops her sketchbook in the dirt and gets up to check her bike. Chains are tight. Tires don't show any signs of wearing. Did she remember to charge the repair kit? Yes, the photovoltaic cells kept reflecting in her eyes while she pedalled. It was sunny today, so everything should be charged. Except for the food printer. She made microalgae dumplings for her hobo stew. Took half the evening to print those. She can recharge it during the ride tomorrow.

Penny leans on her sturdy gravel bicycle. Her eyes trace rippling waves of prairie grass until they fade beyond the light of the fire. In the darkness, not even the horizon can suggest the limits of the plains. Tomorrow, she'll keep looking. Searching. Penny pulls her sleeping bag off her bike and slips into her tent.

• • •

The ride is smooth, despite washboard bumps in the dirt road. The bike's shocks perform their function well. Penny is almost jealous. Things have such defined purposes. They simply are what they are, built well to do what they do. Or at least, they should be. The designer must be up to the task. She must be up to the task. Tension twists in her shoulders.

Slight downhill. Penny takes a slow breath as the road declines, focusing on the whirring of tires. She could've used a mag-lev cycler but she likes the old-school simplicity of the gravel bike, the hum of the spokes. The thoughts clanging around her mind break their confines and drift, floating like clouds. They roll into larger forms, no walls or towers or distractions. Nothing rises to impede them. Nothing gets in their way. Out here, there's enough space for them to untangle and disperse, billowing and rumbling with latent energy. Her design isn't finished yet. There's something still missing. Penny scans the horizon. It's out there, somewhere. A tightness releases from Penny's chest. Beneath her, tires whir.

• • •

Penny bikes, and bikes, and bikes. Dozens of miles. Dozens of sketches. At night she sets up her tent, unfolds the portable food printer and fills it with microalgae solvent or beetroot powder and rainwater. The smart goggles help identify wild plants and herbs to eat. Farmers' markets provide additional nourishment, not to mention the odd roadside diner. People ask about her trip, her destination. She says she doesn't have one. She's just here to explore the prairie, to learn from it. Cycling across the Great Plains. Backroads only. Where all those soulless, self-driving vehicles won't go.

Penny's mind winds as the road twists and turns. There are new discoveries beyond each bend. Her chest heaves during slogs up gravelly hills, problems churning into solutions through forceful cranks of the pedals. Jolts of adrenaline and inspiration punctuate the race back downhill. The journey becomes a dance, a meditation.

The firm wants green solutions. Solar panels. Energy-efficient food printers. Large, immobile edifices. Conventional. Nothing truly radical. Only adaptability rises to meet uncertainty. If Penny wants the partners to consider her proposal, the design must be perfect. Minimalist nomadism provides greater climate resilience. Lower impact. She's miniaturized the tech herself, proving that portable printers and generators can sustain a life in motion. Motion. Momentum. She needs to keep moving. Forward. She's restless at the firm. Directionless. Stuck. She just needs to keep going. Keep pedalling. Just one perfect design. Learn from the prairie. Architecture should inhabit place. Lines. Horizontal lines. Space. Ornamentation is a distraction. Simple motifs. Lines. Divergent, coming together. Lines, lots of

—gravel skids under her tires as she squeezes her brakes. An alarm flashes in her smart goggles. It mirrors the sign on the fence blocking the road. Private Property. No Trespassing.

• • •

Penny follows the fence, grimacing. Half a day wasted, trying to find a way around it. The fence persists, unyielding. Tumbleweeds shaking against the barbed wire remind her of fish caught in a net. The fence looms, seeming to draw closer, constricting, squeezing like a python of twisted, pointed steel. Penny's pace increases. Each pump of the pedal comes faster than the last, until she is racing the fence, feet pumping, heart pounding. She needs to escape, beyond its stifling restrictions, beyond limitations, conventions, traditions, lack of vision. She cannot handle another roadblock, another detour, another dead end. She feels the fence chasing her. Closing in. Closer. It is nearly upon her. If she can just get around it, she's certain the answers are there, on the other side. Out there, in that open, unrestricted expanse of grassland. It's so close. If she can just get to it.

Penny pedals and pedals and pedals and pedals and pedals and pedals and then skids to a halt and screams, throws her helmet, tears pouring down her cheeks. The partners said no. And no. And no. So many times. Stay in your lane. Head down. She doesn't know where she's going. Where her life is taking her. Her career. How high she can climb that ladder.

Penny gasps through sobs. She can't go any further today. Shoulders drooping, resigned, she sets up her tent, her campfire, food printer, water condenser. She sits on the ground. Her sketchbook lies next to her, unopened. Maybe she'll just go to sleep. Penny looks at her tent. She looks at the fence. She looks at her tent.

Homes were not always things that blocked off the natural world. Outdoor and indoor, not antonyms. Not fences. Elements of the same. Sides of a coin in constant rotation. In. Out. Seamless. She can't just adjust the scale of architecture. She needs to rebel against the very concept of sedentary architecture itself.

Penny opens to a new page, and begins to sketch new lines.

• • •

An alarm flashes in the goggles. No Trespassing. Penny opens her backpack, removes the repair kit. There are still lessons she needs to learn from the prairie. She cannot master these teachings if she accepts restriction. Lines fill her mind. Once disparate, they are finding order, harmony, direction.

Architecture should inhabit place. Place should inhabit architecture. The partners will never approve her project. She'll do it on her own. Her own firm. Her own movement. Innovation is rebellious. The prairie is rebellious. It doesn't care about property or jurisdiction or fences. The prairie storms and blows and sweeps and rises and turns, compelled by its own sense of chaos, its own order, its own logic. She was never going to achieve this without risk. Rebellious, defiant, risk. This will challenge conventions, laws, everything. Resilience is radical; transience, revolutionary. Property is conventional. Antiquated. Inequitable. Intolerable. The lines on the horizon and lines in her mind converge. The alarm flashes in her heads-up display. No Trespassing. Penny removes her goggles. She stares at the fence. There's one line that's out of place. She opens the repair kit and withdraws the chain cutter.

Some lines need to be crossed.

# ABOUT THE AUTHOR

Christopher R. Muscato is a writer, adjunct history instructor, and graduate of the Terra.do climate activism fellowship program. He is the former writer-in-residence of the High Plains Library District and a winner of the inaugural XR Wordsmith Solarpunk Storytelling Showcase. His climate fiction can be found scattered throughout the internet.

# HAIKU

## Lisa Taylor

a wave of sadness
where water once flowed freely
only sand remains

# ABOUT THE AUTHOR

Lisa Taylor is an academic librarian and writer with wide-ranging interests. Her poems, essays, articles, and short stories have appeared in print and online in journals and anthologies. She makes her home in Florida, the land of flowers, where it's harder to stop something from growing than to start it.

# PITY THE SQUONK

## Kathryn Yelinek

> THE range of the squonk is very limited.
> —William T. Cox, *Fearsome Creatures*
> *of The Lumberwoods*

The woods were my sanctuary, my cathedral, and goodness knows I needed a refuge that spring. Every day brought more bad news: the hottest April on record, the worst flooding since Hurricane Agnes, unprecedented tree die-offs. A forest ranger could only do so much by herself, and by late May I couldn't stomach another overtime shift. I took my weary bones and heavy heart to the cabin.

Friday night found me curled up on the porch swing with a mug of hot tea, listening to robins settling in for the night. Their calls should have soothed me. That's why I'd come. Instead, I was jittery, almost spilling my tea. I'd driven past a new clear-cut, courtesy of an imminent new pipeline, and the ugly scar through the trees wouldn't leave my mind. Protests and legal manoeuvrings hadn't stopped it, and frustration skittered through my veins. I was so tired. Then, from the shadows between oak and maple, came the sound of weeping.

It was pitiful. A soft keening like someone whose heart was breaking. The sound brought with it the memory of everyone and everything I'd ever loved and lost. I slapped a hand over my mouth before a sob could emerge. My throat felt hot and narrow.

There was no room for fear amid the grief. Yes, I was a young woman alone in a cabin in the middle of the woods. No one should have been out there, certainly no one close enough for me to witness their mourning. But that weeping sounded heartbreaking, not threatening.

More than that, it felt natural, organic, as if it had grown among these trees.

With that thought, the pieces fell into place. The squonk. Of course.

I grabbed my sneakers and shoved them on as quietly as I could while hurrying off the porch. If you're not from Pennsylvania, you may never have heard of the squonk. I first heard of them here in this cabin. My grandmother spoke of them over chamomile tea and raisin cookies. Pity the squonk, she said. They're gentle, shy creatures of the forest. Creatures of twilight, dusk, and dawn. Creatures so ugly they hide and weep out of shame over their own ugliness.

Even as a six-year-old, obsessed with birds and beetles, I knew that didn't make sense. Cryptid or not, no species collectively thinks it's ugly. Somewhere, a female squonk thought a male squonk was quite the catch. Otherwise, they would have gone extinct. Weeping must be their natural sound, which, as usual, we humans misunderstood.

They have always been a rare sight, even among the lumberjacks in the 1800s who first reported them. Still, that elusiveness rankled. Even though I was Pennsylvania born and bred, even though I had been a birdwatcher since age five, and even though I'd worked for the local forest district my entire professional life and logged more hours in the field than some of my older colleagues, I have never seen a squonk. I shouldn't have taken it personally.

I shouldn't, but I did. This time, I would see one.

The weeping came through soft and clear through the trees. I was in luck.

I tramped west, toward the state road, before I realized the sound came from more to the north. I paused, reoriented myself. I followed the noise, keeping my footfalls soft.

It was a good night to be out. The rain had stopped, and moonlight filtered through the young leaves. The forest remained awake as the night settled in, birds winging to their roosts, frogs calling for love. I trod on damp mayapples and fading trout lilies, the mud thick underfoot. Even where branches blocked the moonlight, I wasn't afraid in these woods. I'd walked them many times before. This was my family's land. It knew me, and I knew it. I only feared spooking the elusive squonk.

I stepped wrong on a fallen branch. It cracked underfoot,

too loud.

I froze. I held my breath.

As the crack faded, the forest stayed quiet. Too quiet. The weeping had stopped.

Dang it. The squonk was as skittish as I'd been told.

There was nothing to do but wait and hope. My body was tired, my soul, too, yet I never once thought to head home. Sighting the squonk would do more to feed my soul than another couple hours in bed. I could wait. I held myself still, breathing shallowly, and sent up a prayer to whatever would listen.

Silence.

Slowly, softly, frogs took up their love songs. A mockingbird called. I waited. I hoped.

There. Soft and unmistakable, a muted, pitiful keening.

Back to the west. But now I, too, became wary and skittish. I trod more slowly and carefully. I took out my phone, engaged its red light so I wouldn't ruin my night vision, and recorded thirty seconds of the weeping. With luck, the squonk would respond to a playback of its call, like some birds did. With luck, it would come to me instead of me having to go to it.

I hit "play" and sent my recording into the night.

The weeping stopped, leaving only the artificial sobs.

Double dang it. Another wrong move. I stopped the playback.

But before I could despair, the weeping resumed. Closer. Louder.

I inched forward, careful where I placed my feet, and there in front of me stood a squat, four-legged beast, sobbing at the edge of the new clear-cut.

I stopped, gazing at it, digging my fingers into my thigh to convince myself that I really was seeing it.

To be clear, the clear-cut was the uglier of the two things: a scar of tree stumps and churned-up ground devoid of life, an abomination by way of a future natural gas pipeline. In comparison, the squonk was almost cute. It had the homeliness of a naked mole rat, with wrinkly, ill-fitting skin that looked oversized.

Not cute like a panda, but nothing to cry over. I would take it home for a pet, if it were in an animal rescue.

The squonk wept softly, and as I watched, bathed in the joy of a new sighting, it struck me again that this squonk could not be weeping over its own ugliness. There was no pool of still water or mirror in sight. Neither did it act like a creature calling for love. It wasn't strutting or advertising a possible nest site.

No, there was something more subtle going on. As I stood and watched, I realized its gaze was fixed as firmly on the travesty of the clear-cut as my gaze was fixed on the wonder of a squonk.

I'm a scientist. I deal in data, measurements, and replicable results. Despite that, looking at the squonk, I knew without a doubt, in the mammalian center of my gut, that the squonk grieved the cutting of the forest. That's what it was weeping over.

Now my grandmother's story made sense. The clear-cut explained why the lumberjacks who decimated the Pennsylvania forests heard the squonk when no one else did. Why they assumed it wept over its own ugliness. Those lumberjacks were projecting the ugly work they did onto the humble squonk.

"I'm so sorry," I whispered.

The squonk spun to face me. Tears glittered in its eyes.

I expected it to run. It didn't. Its gaze met mine. It held the sadness of everyone and everything that could be lost.

I wept, too, and went and sat beside it. We sat in tearful solidarity. The two of us, weeping for what had been done to these forests, what was being done, and what would soon be done.

"I'm doing my best to stop it," I said. "I'm just one person. I can only do my small part. But I'll keep trying. I won't stop."

At my words, the squonk bent its head. Its snout touched my knee. An acknowledgement, a benediction.

It turned, no longer weeping, into the forest. It slipped between the mayapples and was gone. I sat a long time in the silence, fingering my phone with the recording. Maybe, just maybe, since the squonk was so rare, this recording would be enough to stop the pipeline. I rose to my feet, ready to continue the good fight.

# ABOUT THE AUTHOR

Kathryn Yelinek lives in Pennsylvania, where she works as a librarian. Her fiction has appeared in *Daily Science Fiction*, *Deep Magic*, *Metaphorosis*, *Andromeda Spaceways Magazine*, and *Beneath Ceaseless Skies*. She has a fondness for retold fairy tales, hopepunk, and happily ever after. When her nose isn't buried in a book, she's frequently found talking to birds or gazing at the stars.

# YOU ARE MY ENDLING

## Julie Reeser

JONI and I got our first biomorph plasty together when we were sixteen. Small changes at first. Cosmetic over functional. Mom and Dad argued constantly, so I didn't feel too badly that I was probably the final wedge to drive them apart.

Dad supported me. He went on about how when he was young, kids claimed ownership of their bodies with tattoos and piercings. He said it was my body, so I could do what I wanted. That's how Joni felt too, even though her mom thought she'd regret it. I think by then, Joni was angry enough that one more fight with her mom didn't matter. She wanted to prove how serious she was instead of rehashing the same argument. A lot of the other kids were getting scales or fur or snouts. We both got our eyes done.

• • •

Creatures were dying faster than we could catalog when one of the seniors came to school with a rhino horn. We'd all oohed and ahhed and begged to touch it. He warned us about

205

the dangers, but all we heard was the defiance. The last rhino had died a year earlier. An Endling. There'd been plenty of regret, talk of doing better, but it was too late. That's us. Our whole generation defined by too little, too late. The biomorphing gives us an outlet. It's grief-punk. A way to maybe save the last of the last—and ourselves.

• • •

After Joni came home with owl eyes that could no longer cry, no longer roll at her mother in exasperation, suddenly her mom was paying attention. My mom still didn't get it. She'd found another family by then and was about to leave us. I was just glad the fighting would stop. I guess I was sad for the mom I'd wanted, but never had. I think she was sad for the daughter she'd always wanted, but that I couldn't be. I didn't want bouncy hair or designer clothes. I didn't care about boys or gossip. I wanted Joni and a future for us to live in.

"But why an owl? They're so ugly, Samantha. Life is hard enough without being ugly."

Adults aren't supposed to say those things, right? Pretty girls get ahead. Nobody likes a troublemaker. A winning smile is a woman's best asset. She was always life coaching me like I was a client. I hated it.

"They mean death," I'd answered. I'd felt some satisfaction in the recoil she couldn't contain.

"But you don't want to die, do you?"

I tried again. "Think of it like atonement. For your sins. You know, sins of the father, four generations or whatever."

Two lines deepened between her eyes. She'd begun to wrinkle. "So, you're punishing yourself? Punishing me?"

"No, Mom. Atonement. It's not the same thing."

Her wrinkles grew shadows. "It's not?"

She moved out a month later. She sent me pics of her new step-daughter, Cassie. She's very pretty and swims on a team. I sent back that she'd make a fine trout. Mom didn't reply.

• • •

Dad and I talked about the risk before I had the bones done.

"You know you're *my* Endling," he'd said.

"I'm sorry, Dad."

"No, don't be sorry." He shook his head and turned his face from mine. "You aren't the first to try drastic ways to change the world for the better. I just hope you aren't the last."

"It's going to be OK," I'd said. It was an echo of the lie he'd often repeated to me as I was growing up.

He nodded in recognition and did what I had always done. Let it slide.

• • •

The bone plasty was the biggest step with the deepest risk. Joni and I took turns. I went first, and she helped Dad nurse me through the six-month recovery period. When it was finished, I'd felt like an astronaut on the moon. I kept joking I'd float away if someone didn't tie me down. Joni would squeeze me tightly and promise to keep me grounded until we could fly away together. When Dad hugged me, I could feel him searching through my thick feathers to find the girl he once knew. Even though my grafts felt rubbery, he never flinched away.

Then, it was Joni's turn. By then, her mother was more than paying attention—she was leading the charge. She'd been recording Joni's changes on her channel and trying to get a sponsor for a media tour. The trick was in balancing the message between awareness and hope. She'd been contacted by two wildlife refuges, but so far no one was willing to go as far as we were with risk. They all still had corporate donors and fine print that harmed more than it helped. It was frustrating. We were giving up so much, and nothing was changing.

"Maybe that's why they call it grassroots," I'd joked.

Joni laughed, "Right? It's so slow."

Her mom squeezed her hand. "Yeah, but eventually it gets too big to ignore."

• • •

Joni died on the table.

Her biomorpher said it was a fast-rejection of the plasty cells. He'd seen it once before, but never so quick. She went into shock and never recovered.

"Like the salmon in Lake Mead," I'd whispered.

Dad says grief does strange things to people. He says I can't fault Joni's mom for not wanting to see me right now. That I'm a reminder of what she's lost. Which was our point. Why is it so easy to grieve one but not the save the whole?

Joni would never have wanted to be embalmed and put in

the dirt. She wanted to fly.

• • •

I know Dad heard me sneak out, but he didn't stop me. The media is covering the funeral. Joni's death is sensational where her life wasn't, just like an Endling's. All the biomorphed kids in our horns, feathers, elytra, and hides will be there. Ugly activists causing trouble. My mother will be horrified.

## ABOUT THE AUTHOR

Julie Reeser is the author of three poetry chapbooks and the novella *Language of the Spirit*. Her short fiction can be found in *The Dread Machine*, *Bourbon Penn*, and others. Her Patreon churns out small quirks and weekly words, and she's obsessed with discovering comfortable seating and the best verbs. There's a cool carousel of stories you can ride on her website — www.persephoneknits.com. She is disabled, but not done.

# THE FIRST AND LAST CONCERT OF AVALONIA JEMISON'S PEACE LILY

## Matt Bliss

AVALONIA Jemison walks into the Plaza restaurant only a day before the event, wearing the brisk confidence usually reserved for politicians and the like, but the midseventies retiree carries it better than most. This is impressive when considering she's also carrying the potted houseplant I'm here to interview.

She places the plant on the barstool across from me and seats herself beside it. When the waitress takes our orders, she says, "Only water," and flashes me a wry smile. One leg folds over another and she interlocks her hands in her lap as if she has been preparing her whole life for this interview. The world was waiting, no doubt.

"Does it have a name?" I ask, feeling foolish for doing so, but this simple fact had yet to come out in the barrage of internet and tabloid headlines. I'd done my research, everyone had, but despite having experience interviewing politicians and celebrities, one is never quite prepared to interview a houseplant.

"No name." Avalonia switches her tone to something bordering on irritation. "They have asked that all lines of questioning be directed to them. The agreement was not for *me* to be interviewed." She gestures toward the deep green mess of leaves beside her. "I'm only … the translator, I suppose."

I raise a skeptical brow. "*They* told you that, did they?"

Avalonia's smile never falters. "Yes. *They* did."

"Right." I quickly apologize and turn toward the plant.

Avalonia, perhaps, is what makes this story even more intriguing. Moments like these are frequent among our interview, and even knowing the MIT studies, brain wave readouts, and neurological scans, I can't help but feel like she is putting me on. Avalonia, whether she thinks so or not, is the foundation of this story. The peace lily had chosen to communicate with her and her alone. The designated telepathic mouthpiece to the world. Moreover, while researchers had concluded there was nothing special about her brain—that the plant *chooses* to communicate with only her—as I sit across from her it is easy to see why she was selected.

I can't help but feel like she is inside my own head.

Reading my thoughts, whispering hushed words. I ask myself what it would feel like for her or a plant to do just that. I pause and search for something there, probing me, but feel nothing. No sense of an organic something reaching into my head and plucking neurons like guitar strings. Instead, all I feel is awkward.

"Let's get right to it then," I say to the plant, detecting no discernable difference or movement in its leaves. "You are the first of your kind, or at least the first we are aware of. Can all plants communicate like this, or is it only you? And what is it about Avalonia that you chose to communicate with her?" My eyes bounce between her and the plant.

Avalonia locks her eyes on me. "They wish not to answer," she says. "They …" Avalonia blinks rapidly and turns her head just a tick. "They have called you here to make an announcement."

Again, even in this gravely serious moment I can't help but feel I'm being taken advantage of.

"An announcement?" I ask. "What announcement?"

"Tomorrow," she continues. "They will reach out to whoever will listen. They will reach out with a message."

"And what is the message?"

"Tomorrow," she says and places the glass to her lips. She smiles behind it and raises her brows. "Tomorrow."

• • •

A hesitant anticipation buzzes through the Roosevelt Theatre as the last seats are filled. It's as fitting a place for this spectacle as any. History feels alive within this hundred-and-thirty year-old building, so what better a place to make it? Perhaps a little piece of tonight's magic might seep into these golden walls and arced ceilings so the moment will resonate for eons.

Avalonia looks as radiant as ever as she takes a seat next to me. I ask her if she knows what is to come, but she only gives me a familiar thin-lipped smile.

"It was music at first," Avalonia later tells me when I ask about first discovering the plant speaking in her head. "It sounded like fingers fluttering on piano keys. Changing notes and drawing emotion with sound. Sound only I could hear. I thought I was crazy, but the feeling was so strong I couldn't deny it. It took a long time for the two of us to agree on how to communicate with each other after that."

While the crowd shifts in their seats, waiting for the opportunity to have this plant slither into their minds, I can't help but consider the beauty of that statement. Our digital age is rife with dispute, conflict, and societal discourse. A societal norm we have reluctantly come to accept. Yet amongst it, Avalonia and her houseplant have not only unveiled a world of hidden consciousness, but broken other barriers as well. An agreement in communication. Laying ground rules and setting limits. This is perhaps yet another reason why Avalonia was chosen.

"I think it's because I was listening." Avalonia tells me. "Librarians are used to listening. Taking the bits and pieces of what someone is looking for, reading between the lines in order to help them. That's what it feels like. The plant gives me the pieces and I just have to put them together."

The theatre lights dim at three minutes past the hour, and a hush washes over the crowd. Velvet curtains splay to reveal a squat, rather unremarkable stool at centre stage. Ever so carefully, a black-clad technician walks from stage left, with the peace lily cradled in her arms. There are no microphones. No speakers, sound system, or mixing board, only a potted peace lily placed ever so gently on top of a stool.

The room leans closer in unison. Inspecting the slight droop of its leaves and the bone-white flowers stretching from its centre. Everyone anxious to feel this houseplant speak into their mind.

Avalonia reaches a hand over to my own and squeezes. Her face is soft when I turn to her, tears glistening from both her wrinkled cheeks, yet not a hint of sadness remains. Instead, she beams like a proud parent. I reciprocate the gesture, and turn back to the potted plant sitting centre stage of a packed auditorium, and together, the room waits.

The voice that comes next, the one that shakes the world, is not a voice at all, but music.

Reports will vary wildly from this point in the night. Each individual claims to have experienced it differently, but from one person to the next there is one constant within the stories. The connection between us all is the music.

It is not like speech or even text for that matter, but only describable as a connection. A handhold so intimate and encompassing it defies explanation. It searches you, cocoons you while probing within your centre. And within there, you find a sound. The sound of life and death and light and dark and everything yet nothing, resonating within you as if *you* are now the instrument. We all are in this symphony of existence.

Without a doubt, *this* is the message.

No reaction feels inappropriate among the 3875 in attendance. Some cry. Some stand rigid and stoic in their seats. Some rise with arms spread wide and chins raised to the heavens. Some fall to their knees, or scream as if on fire, but the message is clear.

The music finally fades, and the peace lily's warm tendril of thought slides free from our minds. The crowd calms and turns back toward the stage. We all watch as the first leaf falls —withered and brightening to a sickly yellow—fluttering down to the floor. We all watch, and we know it won't be the last.

Avalonia has slipped away at some point during the plant's performance. I wait as the place clears out, hoping she'll come back, but she never returns.

In that time, however, I watch as total strangers become friends. People bond over something they will spend the rest of their lives trying to explain. They hold one another, shake hands, smile, cry, and for the first time in some of their lives, agree on how to communicate with one another. Time is a fleeting thing, and as the world turns back toward that gilded stage, watching, waiting for the last leaf to fall, or for the peace lily to speak to us once again, we must ask ourselves, *how long? Where will we be?* But perhaps most importantly, who will be there to hold your hand when the last leaf falls?

# ABOUT THE AUTHOR

Matt Bliss is a construction worker turned speculative fiction writer from Las Vegas, Nevada. His short fiction has appeared in *Diabolical Plots*, *MetaStellar*, and *Etherea Magazine*, among other published and forthcoming works. When he's not attempting to telepathically communicate with his houseplants, you can find him on Twitter at @MattJBliss.

# ABOUT THE EDITOR

KATRINA Archer is the author of dark fantasy *The Tree of Souls* and YA fantasy *Untalented,* a *Library Journal* Indie Ebook Award Honorable Mention. A former software engineer, she has worked in aerospace, video games, and film, and is a freelance copy editor and publisher of climate change site *Little Blue Marble.* She can operate almost any vehicle that can't fly, doesn't believe in life without books or chocolate, and together with her spouse, puts up with the antics of a sweet potato and a chaos goblin masquerading as cats. Connect with her online at www.katrinaarcher.com.

For more great fiction and features about
our changing climate, join us at

*LittleBlueMarble.ca*

**Also available from** *Little Blue Marble:*

*Little Blue Marble 2022: Warmer Worlds*

*Little Blue Marble 2021: Tipping Points*

*Little Blue Marble 2020: Greener Futures*

*Little Blue Marble 2019: Climate in Crisis*

*Little Blue Marble 2018: More Stories of Our
Changing Climate*

*Little Blue Marble 2017: Stories of Our
Changing Climate*